W9-CNA-674

When Trying to
Return Home

When Trying to Return Home

❋ STORIES ❋

Jennifer Maritza McCauley

Counterpoint
Berkeley, California

When Trying to Return Home

Copyright © 2023 by Jennifer Maritza McCauley
First hardcover edition: 2023

All rights reserved under domestic and international copyright. Outside of fair use (such as quoting within a book review), no part of this publication may be reproduced, stored in a retrieval system, or transmitted in any form or by any means, electronic, mechanical, photocopying, recording, or otherwise, without the written permission of the publisher. For permissions, please contact the publisher.

This book is a work of fiction. Names, characters, places, and incidents are the product of the author's imagination or are used fictitiously. Any resemblance to actual events is unintended and entirely coincidental.

Names: McCauley, Jennifer Maritza, author.
Title: When trying to return home : stories / Jennifer Maritza McCauley.
Description: First hardcover edition. | Berkeley, California : Counterpoint Press, 2023.
Identifiers: LCCN 2022038679 | ISBN 9781640095687 (hardcover) | ISBN 9781640095694 (ebook)
Subjects: LCSH: African Americans—Fiction. | Black people—Fiction. | LCGFT: Short stories.
Classification: LCC PS3613.C3568925 W47 2023 | DDC 813/.6—dc23/ eng/20220819
LC record available at https://lccn.loc.gov/2022038679

Jacket design and illustration by Jaya Miceli
Book design by Laura Berry

COUNTERPOINT
2560 Ninth Street, Suite 318
Berkeley, CA 94710
www.counterpointpress.com

Printed in the United States of America

10 9 8 7 6 5 4 3 2 1

To Abba, my family, and Jesse

Perhaps home is not a place but simply an irrevocable condition.

—JAMES BALDWIN,
GIOVANNI'S ROOM

Contents

When Trying to Return Home

Torsion

WHEN I WAS A TEEN GIRL, MY HIGH SCHOOL TEACHER came up to my mother. That teacher, all pink-pocked and smiling, told my mama I was going to do something good with my life. *Your girl looks straight forward*, she said. *She'll see success, for sure.* That woman, whoever she was, was wrong as hell.

If Mama's plan to snatch her son from White Nurse worked, she and I would be criminals. Baby snatchers. Dark-skinned derelicts. We'd be the dead-eyed Black folks they throw up on KDKA after a story about recalled strollers. If the news story was longer than a clip, the announcers might roll through our supposedly hoodrat attributes. Mama: a be-weaved hair technician who barely made rent at our apartment on the Hill, who had two kids from two different daddies.

She was a PTA at Allegheny General for years and a terrific stylist, but those bits didn't make the story simple. Me: a part-time Eat N' Park waitress (I was a college student at Point Park, but would they mention that?) who made the *Gazette* once for saying, "He wasn't all bad," about her ex-boyfriend who'd robbed a Texaco. If Mama's plan didn't work, the five o'clock news would be fast to break us down as they saw fit. The St. Benedict ladies would frown at the screen and suck their teeth. My professors would shrug and delete my name from their rosters. Parker, the schizophrenic who slept in our apartment and sort of loved Mama, would think about helping us but give up halfway through the thought. The boy I loved would shake his head and say, "There you go, like I've always said. She could never say no to her mama."

So, you see, my mother and I couldn't fail.

At four o'clock in the morning, I backed my mother's slug-colored minivan out of the Banford Dwellings parking lot. My hands, sweat-wet and sticky, slid down the wheel. I stamped on the brakes, stopped at the mouth of the lot.

I rested my forehead against the wheel. The sky reddened above the shadows of rust-colored tenements, dollar marts, and fading apartment complexes. A knob of moonlight sunk underneath the arms of the St. Benedict statue, which stood drearily atop our orange-bricked church. Crows cawed in poplar trees I couldn't see; the 83 cracked gravel as it rolled on to the next bus stop.

At 4:00 a.m., in mid-November, I was still a good-enough person. My definition of myself: a junior in college, an awkward girl who played varsity softball and took weekend rides on Allegheny riverboats. I was someone who could still do something nice with her life.

I looked at Mama. My mother stared forward at the street, her naked lips stitched in a stiff line. Her eyes were wrenched wide. Her hair was greased against her scalp; her skin fresh smelling and slathered with baby oil. She wore whitewashed jeans and a green shirt that clutched her muscle-strong arms. Her hands were folded in her lap. I tried not to look too hard at her; her calm body made me nervous. My whole life that woman had made me nervous with love for her. She told me no matter what I was her only Thing; she told me—when the schoolkids called me strange because of my stutter and crooked nose—that I'd always have her. So I was hers.

After a few moments, when I didn't move the van, Mama tapped my wrist.

"Claudia," she said. "You can't get sick on me. You sick?"

I shook my head and licked my lips. Icy feelings shot back and forth in my hands.

"You eat something 'fore we left? I didn't see you," she said.

I nodded.

"What you eat?"

"Macaroni," I lied. I hadn't eaten a thing because I hadn't slept the whole night wondering if we'd pull this off, and when I didn't sleep I wasn't hungry.

"I don't believe you ate that pasta."

"You didn't see me," I admitted. I swallowed hard. I should have brought water with me; Mama was right. My mouth was dry, lips already burning.

"*Baby.* Eat a sandwich. It'll calm you. Made you three for when we get to Morgantown, and you can't help me with no strength. Your sandwiches are in the red cooler, under the clothes for Sam. They labeled with your name on them. Check: Egg salad. Chicken salad. Look: roast beef."

"Mama," I said carefully, looking at the road. "If you want me to drive, please don't ask me to eat something. I'm going to throw it up."

Mama clenched her jaw. "I'm trying—to take care of you."

"Not hungry."

Mama blew air from her nose. She leaned over and rubbed circles into the back of my neck. "Too much worrying in you. Sweet girl. Things are gonna be straight. 'Do not worry.' That's a commandment from Jesus. So don't worry."

"That's not a commandment . . . ," I started but stopped myself from going on. I twisted around to get a water bottle from the back seat, but Mama grabbed it for me. She uncapped the top and went on, "Stop worrying. Remember what Mrs. Gonzales said and what the church say. I'm right. We right. God will help the righteous and right. Remember the red on Sam's arms. Keep all that in front of your mind when you drive for me."

Mama handed me the uncapped water. I yanked the bottle from her and drank until my insides felt slippery.

"Sure," I said. I didn't feel better.

Those were the "rights" Mama kept in her head, the things she repeated to herself like a sacred prayer. Those things: The social worker who approached Mama after the doctors left and said, "Mrs. Gibson, you took care of Sam very well. You never forget that. He shouldn't have been taken from you." The St. Benedict church ladies who hugged Mama and said, "Phoenix, you a good mother. The Lord sees how you loved your boy." There was Danni, Mama's longtime friend, a Polish American woman who worked at the DMV and got us White Nurse's address in Aliquippa. Danni believed in Mama so much she drove by White Nurse's house to check out my little brother's situation every week. Danni told Mama she saw the woman cussing at Sam when he played outside, saw White Nurse slapping him and pulling the blinds closed afterward. Danni said when White Nurse was out, she'd go up to the window and peer in, check the house plans, look for signs of fault, and she'd see them. Many. Danni said: "I don't trust that nurse, Phee. I smell abuse. You get your Sam back. He's yours. Blood trump law."

I couldn't convince Mama that she was committing a True Crime by stealing my brother back from his foster mother, so I didn't. Mama put me through college; she reminded me often of how she went broke paying for my education, and she was right. I loved my mama more than morality, and the Law couldn't challenge my love for her.

I took my foot off the brake.

Mama picked a little pimple underneath her ear. "It's

early. Maybe the travel time you got on the website will be cut in half. Maybe we'll get there early. No traffic on 376. But we should get going anyway. You don't want to have to do nothing to that woman, if the time off. You'll have to, but—"

"I'm going," I said. I didn't want to think about knocking White Nurse out. That would never be part of my plan. It was always part of Mama's.

I palmed the wheel to the left and mouthed "goodbye" to our four-story apartment building. Nobody slept well at Banford Dwellings. A punched-in window on the third floor revealed our neighbor Keets Pattie looking at our GMC, his stomach damp and hair-coated. He scratched his shivering breasts, shut his eyes, and stumbled back to his computer screen. Couples in studios on Crawford were hollering hate, shiny Black ladies in night bonnets growled to ghosts in their sleep, shivering gentrifiers were smoking crack and watching Looney Tunes. Silverware slammed and crashed; chairs scratched lines across floors. T. D. Jakes bellowed from stereos, late-night television ads talked about ellipticals and big-mouthed juicers and how you could change your life in thirty days if you fastened a trainer to your stomach that shook until you got fit.

I'd never hear these sounds again.

I knew Parker, Mama's boyfriend, was still in bed, his nose smashed against Mama's pillow. The noodle-haired white man hadn't heard us leave the apartment and we didn't tell him our plans. When he woke up and read Mama's one-word goodbye note, he'd yowl. He'd punch the wall, hurl the lamp, dump the contents of cereal boxes on the kitchen floor. He'd curl up on the couch and blame wriggling demons, the government conspirators, and the biblical animals that kept his brain company. He'd throw his medicines in the toilet to spite Mama; he'd attempt suicide, decide against it, and attempt it again. Parker was sleeping now, but he was dead already. We weren't criminals yet, but we'd killed Parker the moment we pulled out of the apartment.

I turned onto Chauncey and blew out a long breath. I passed the waving trees, broken at mid-bend, the patches of yellowed grass separating stuck-together buildings. I passed Hot Cuts, where Sam used to get his shape-ups; I passed the repair shop where Mama fixed our groaning axel. I drove by the razed buildings from the "urban renewal movement," the trash-bag-filled alleyways, and the corner where my friends Kick and Dowl busked with a Casio and bass. August Wilson made poetry of our city's jitneys and barbershops, our con men and baseball players, our playboys and weeping mothers. If I squinted hard enough I could still see that poetry, but I couldn't look at the Hill anymore. I had to go forward.

I kept my eyes on the road and pushed the van past the PPG Building with its many-mirrored walls, past the fountain in its plaza. My college classes were in a warehouse nearby Point Park, and I didn't want to see the place. Last week, my boyfriend and I had played in PPG's pulsing fountain-water. He chased me, I chased him. I grabbed the back of his shirt and he turned around and lifted me in the air. Last week, he drove me to the Carnegie Library and then we studied for a marketing test in his dorm. That night, I'd told him, "I don't have enough planned out." He pushed his lips into my neck and said, "You've got this. You'll pass." I didn't say anything. He said, "What's enough? What's wrong?" I said, "This'll be a disaster." He thought I was talking about the exam; I wasn't. He didn't like when I talked about my mother, so I didn't talk about her. I didn't tell him I wasn't coming back; he'd find out soon enough.

Mama told me it was all right to leave the city now that I'd finished my junior year. *You can finish your degree in Jacksonville,* she'd promised. *When we get there, after we get set up, you'll finish,* she'd said. *Just one more year.*

I wiped my eyelids with my left hand. I wasn't going to cry but my eyelids throbbed. I looked at Mama. Her face didn't give up anything. Her eyes were half-closed; she licked her teeth slowly. I couldn't see the lines of Mama's face well, just the profile of her mouth and the feathery shadow of her eyelashes. What was she feeling? I couldn't figure it out. She'd met my papi, a Puerto Rican man named Alfonso, in this city. They'd both been barbacks at Garage Door in Oakland, fell for each other fast but agreed on a temporary affair. Alfonso was on a break from his boyfriend in New York, and Mama was done with her PTA position and wanted to start cosmetology school without too much fuss. Eventually, Papi told her he was going to marry the man from New York, so they broke up for good. Mama and my father decided to stay just-friends, even after she accidentally got pregnant with me.

It didn't take her long to get over Alfonso, she said, because he was so kind and honest and he hadn't tried to trick or hurt her. Even now, she said, he was the best man she'd ever met. My father always sent his payments; he picked up the phone to talk to me if I needed someone. I hadn't called my father to discuss Mama's plan, though, this crime. He'd be mortified. And there was Sam's daddy, that awful Martin Malls. She'd met him here too, on the 72A. She near-died loving him. I understood why she wouldn't miss Pittsburgh, if any part of the city reminded her of Martin. But still. There were memories. I didn't understand how she could leave Pittsburgh so blithely. This city where she'd given Sam her kidney, even though his little body rejected her parts.

She remembered, didn't she? Did she wonder, at all, if we were doing the right thing? Even bad memories were still memories. And yet, my mama looked at the window, her face blank, almost bored.

"We're getting on 376," I said, hoping Mama would twitch. "You're right. There's not going to be any traffic."

"Good."

I swallowed down a croak and said, "We can't come back to Pittsburgh, Mama."

If it wasn't Mama's home, it was mine. Even if we successfully stole my brother and his dialysis machine from White Nurse, we could never return. Sam's machine belonged to the state; it was assigned a traceable code. We had to stay off the grid, which was as far away from Pittsburgh as we could.

Mama didn't say much more. The engine grunted and

coughed up smog. She didn't smell fresh anymore. The old coffee in Mama's mouth stank, the funk of her armpits crowded the van. The wiper blades cleared the condensation from the windshield.

Mama turned her head to the left. She pulled her lips into her mouth and pushed them out. She ran a hand over the back of my braids.

"Claudia," she said. "Let me tell you something. I've lived my whole life giving myself to you. Monday through Sunday. You and Sam why I work, why I haven't shot myself dead. I may have given too many of my everydays to Parker, too many to Martin, but even on those days I was living for you. Believe me, if you wanted my hair or bone or skin, I'd yank any of it off my body and give it to you. Sam got my kidney. I'd give you my heart too."

"I'm not saying you aren't giving enough . . . ," I started. I didn't want to hear about this kind of love.

Mama held up her hand. She pointed a long-nailed finger to her back, where the kidney she gave Sam used to be. "Stomach, spleen, heart-blood. I don't care if doctors won't let me give it. I'll tear any piece of me off and shove it in your body. You know this."

"Mama . . ."

She laid her fingers on my arm. Her hand felt wooden, cold. "I'm asking you to do one thing for me, Claudia. That's it. When you said yes, my heart was so full I couldn't know no greater happiness."

I kept my face mask-like, my biceps tensed, my insides

tight. Mama was speaking her truth. It was a hard truth, and it was hard for me to hear. But to me, as a kid and even as a young woman, her truth always felt true. When I was a little girl, boys bullied me because of my shaky stare, stutter, and overbite. Mama would call me the prettiest girl she'd even seen, tell me that I could say anything and my voice would sound like a song. Anytime Mama saw me crying in my room alone after class, she came to school the next day and cussed out the teachers and the students. When the soccer boy threw his hand on my vagina while I was trying to teach him trig, I told Mama and she called the school, again. When they didn't do anything, she left a message on that boy's voice mail every day for a week saying she knew guys that'd put a hole in his head. She got him on the phone and said stuff I didn't hear, but he showed up at my homeroom on his knees, weeping his apologies. Mama put me in better schools with sweeter teachers; she was my only friend through multiple breakups and tear-filled nights and cold days. She saved all her money for my college education because she believed in me, believed I wasn't too slow or ugly or soft-spoken to be forgotten. I applied and got into Point Park because of my mama. I never really wanted to be in college anyway, I told myself; I just wanted to please my mama, my only friend. I wanted to pay her back for all of her love.

So, you see, I was trapped.

———

The thing is, Mama never loved neat. Her love was spread out, sloppy. It slathered everyone in her path and she didn't care how it hit or who it hurt, as long as she was giving it.

I've always seen her the same way: twirling in the field behind Banford, her arms outstretched, eyes huge. Like an overeager saint, holy light spit from her like knives, blasting through the pores of her body and cutting everyone around her. Everything around her was subsumed and stabbed by all that Mama-love, but no light would touch her.

Maybe she shouldn't have met that Martin Malls, Sam's daddy. Mama loved Sam's daddy with the worst kind of love. The sort of love that gets sludge-thick, that dirties, sinks, slows a body to quaky immobility. On her thirty-ninth birthday, she met that Martin Malls on the city bus and that new, bleak love rushed in and ruined all her clear thought. Martin was Mama's age and a manager at the UPS Store downtown. He had panther-soft skin, high cheekbones, and a hard torso. He had been married before but treated Mama like she was his gift, a personal reward after his disastrous former marriage. He was attracted to Mama's matronly spirit, all her slathery giving, and they fell fast. They were together for a little over a year, up until Sam was born. A month or so after, I came back home from Schenley High and found my mama lying underneath the kitchen table. A folded-up note sat inches away from her fingertips. It was a fast letter, scribbled sloppily. Martin had found another woman, simple as that. Nothing elaborate. He promised to send Sam money and thanked my mother. He told her he might change his mind, but he didn't. He rarely sent money, changed his phone number, and left the state.

Mama was useless for the next few years, and I had to take an extra job to support her while she steadily lost her wages at the salon. My father, on the other hand, was living in Bangladesh with his husband, and he took the time to send extra money for all of us, but he was running low and Mama blew through his checks fast. He promised to help us out but needed time.

Meanwhile, Mama found Martin online. She messaged him and he responded, surprisingly, and he started calling her every other week, insisting he felt guilty. He started trying again: he wanted pictures of Sam and he sent some checks to us. Then he faded away and disappeared completely by Sam's third birthday, the year Sam was diagnosed with renal failure. When I left a message on Martin's phone to tell him Mama was about to give up her kidney for their son, Mama was sure he'd leave his girl. That he'd come back to Pittsburgh, speed to the hospital and throw open the doors just when Mama was about to be cut open. Like the men in the movies that have a change of heart. She thought he'd declare his love and clutch her hand and weep by her side, that he'd finally realize she was his precious One. He didn't show up, blocked Mama from his social media, and got another new phone number. After the transplant, Mama got pit-low and started overloving everything to make up for her lack of love. She brought in Parker, a sixty-year-old gray-skinned groundskeeper who could see people we couldn't see, and she put all her affection into him. Despite all the imaginary people Parker could see, he looked through my mother. He just liked her sandwiches, sex, and special care.

Sam lost the kidney because of torsion. Mama's organ had twisted in Sam's body, cut off his blood supply. Her kidney was too heavy for Sam to carry. After he went on dialysis, she should have kicked Parker out. She should have stopped the extra work. She should have reexamined her life, but she didn't. She kept loving Sam, kept loving me, kept loving Parker and her clients and everyone with all that too-much love that blinded and drained my mama so much, it stopped achieving its purpose. She didn't notice we were getting sick from her love. I was losing weight, Parker was losing his mind, Sam had lost his kidney. Nobody had enough money. Mama didn't notice the rodents trickling into the apartment, the times Sam cried out to Parker that his "insides" hurt, the times Parker just sat on the couch, watching the ceiling, not helping at all. And Mama and I worked, worked, worked. She didn't notice the squalor, but our landlord did and he called Child and Youth Services.

Mama didn't notice her kind of love was cruel until CYS took my brother. Maybe she could have turned her life anew, but she didn't. She wanted to prove to Sam she could love him right this time, and now she was using me to steal him back. I could have had a revelation about Mama before all this; I could have thought: my perfect mother is going to hurt me too.

But I didn't. I could never say no to my mama.

———

Twenty minutes after we left the Hill, I parked our van in front of White Nurse's redbrick ranch house. It was a one-story, with a wraparound white wood porch. Even though it was late November, Halloween skeletons and pumpkin stickers were stuck in the windows; it looked kid-friendly. It looked like it smelled like citrus slices and white-people things. A wreath of plastic harvest leaves hung on the front door. It was a lovely house, humble and well-kept. Sam was inside, but it wasn't Sam's house. Mama was right.

Inside, my baby brother wheezed next to the humming dialysis machine. Inside, White Nurse was dreaming about the things White Nurses dreamed about.

I carved lines up and down the wheel with my finger. The drive had gone by too fast. I didn't want to be here so soon, at this perfect place.

Mama slid her eyes over at me. "Ready?"

I scratched the spaces between my plaits. The itchiness got bigger, meaner, and I imagined a little mosquito sucking away all the blood in my head. Of course I wasn't ready.

Mama said, "Magnetized box in the mailbox, Danni say. Danni say White Nurse's room on the left side of the living room; Sam's room is on the right. Danni say White Nurse sleep with the door shut. We go in together to Sam's room. You keep watch while I unhook him from the machine."

I knew the plan. We'd gone over it before. I'd carry the machine and get the dialysate boxes; Mama would carry Sam out and snatch any other supplies. If White Nurse came in while Mama was working, I had to knock her out. No other choice. We'd get in the van, drive to Morgantown where Danni's friends were, stay there for the rest of the day, dialyze Sam at night. We'd move on to Charlestown the next day, stay with Danni's other friends there, dialyze Sam at night. On the third day, we'd get to Jacksonville, where Mama's sister lived. We'd start a new life there, with Sam. Mama said the plan could work; there were success stories. Mama had found these stories in online newspapers, of mamas who'd taken their babies back. She read about families who took their sick kids out of state and weren't found for years. There were success stories.

We pulled on some child-size gloves Mama'd bought from the dollar store. Mama didn't want to leave fingerprints, but I was pretty sure we'd be the first suspects for the crime, so who cared?

"Wait. Let's just wait," I said, my pulse throbbing in my forehead. Couldn't I turn around, go back to my boyfriend and school? In the van, now, right now, I wasn't a criminal.

"Wait for what? How long you need?"

"I don't know. Let me think."

"About *what*?"

"Mama . . ."

"Two minutes," Mama said crisply. She crossed her arms and stared hard at White Nurse's house. I shook my head. I couldn't control my legs; I was snapping my knees, and my ankles shivered.

We stayed in the van for a few minutes, listening to the morning sounds in this clean neighborhood. I gnawed on my lips. I couldn't imagine going against my mama. I had to help her. She'd given me everything, like she'd said.

"All right," Mama said.

"Okay," I croaked. I turned the van off.

Mama and I opened our doors at the same time.

We padded softly across the empty street, across White Nurse's well-washed sidewalk and up her wooden porch steps. I opened the black steel mailbox attached to the wall near the front door. The magnetized box was inside; White Nurse hadn't moved it. I reached down, pulled out the box, and took out the little bronze key with a kitten sticker. I blinked at the sticker and licked my bottom lip. Maybe now. I could turn around now. I still hadn't started the crime. I could drop the key, grab Mama's hand, wrench her back to our car. Maybe Sam would be okay. The neighborhood was pleasant, the ranch house was better than anything Mama could afford. Maybe Danni was exaggerating or telling Mama what she wanted to hear, maybe Sam wasn't being abused after all. Maybe I could get Mama to wait, find better ways to get her son back.

Mama slapped my skinny shoulder blade. She grabbed the back of my neck, pulled it close to her face. I could smell the Vaseline she'd rubbed on her neckfolds.

She mouthed, "I told you. Be. Calm."

I fluttered my eyes and nodded.

I opened the screen door and slid the key into the lock. Mama held open the screen and we stepped into White Nurse's living room. Watery moonlight flooded curtains hanging long from floor-length windows. We could see the room clearly; it was beautiful: warm cedar walls, plush blood-red carpets, wicker chairs, a flat-screen television, and two high bookshelves with rows of medical and literature books. A fireplace with a painting of bamboo trees sat between a pair of Norfolk pine plants. The room smelled like rosemary petals, roasted nuts, a Christmas too soon.

I pinched the back of Mama's arm. She waved me away. Her nostrils flared; her eyes darted about the angles and curves of the furniture in the living room. She was probably thinking about our apartment's living room, where the landlord discovered Sam on the floor after Parker went through an episode. Mama was rarely home and too exhausted to clean anything but Sam's little space. One afternoon, the landlord found Sam in our living room with his foot cut open from Parker's broken whiskey bottle. After the landlord looked at the grime-smudged floor, the empty cabinets, and the stinkbugs skittering around unwashed dishes, he called CYS. Nobody would flag White Nurse's living room; it was immaculate.

I touched Mama's shoulder again. She jumped up, looked at me with huge, cloudy eyes. Mama shook her head and mouthed, "Sorry, baby. Let's go."

Danni said White Nurse slept on the left side of the living room, Sam on the right. Mama left my side and followed the clicking sound of the dialysis machine to her son's room. She grabbed my wrist and pulled me down a rose-dotted hall-way. Mama stopped at the mouth of Sam's door, sucked in a breath. The clicking sound grew louder and louder; I could hear little-boy gasps. Mama let out a sigh and released my hand. She pushed against the door softly.

Sam's thermal blankets rested on his hips; his teddy bear–print shirt was pulled up to reveal a hump of black stomach. A catheter stretched from the space below his belly button to the machine. His lips were spread apart, his teeth—an assortment of jagged stubs and oblong shapes—gleamed white. He had Martin's round jawline and honey skin, Mama's pushed-out ears and V-shaped eyebrows.

Mama paused, the lines on her forehead scrunching, releasing, tightening. She bit her teeth, cleared her throat.

"My baby is so beautiful," she said.

I looked at my brother, at all his flesh attached to wire, tube, and line. My Sam always looked like half machine, half boy at night. I watched the fluids surge from his stomach to the machine. His lips opened, pursed, opened.

I wiped sweat off my neck with the back of my hand.

I could still go back. I could whip around, sprint out of the house, run down the white-peopled streets until I got to a bus stop. I could take the bus downtown, crash at my boyfriend's place near campus, ignore my mother's calls forever.

Mama turned to me, her eyes bright, face soft.

She nodded.

I gulped, then nodded back. I loved my mama, loved her, loved her.

Mama tiptoed over to Sam's bedside and began the fast work of unhooking the boy safely from the dialysis machine. She removed the tape from his glossy stomach slowly, rubbing his left leg to keep him calm. When she removed the catheter, Sam's eyes snapped open and he looked down at Mama's black head. He said, "Ma . . . ?" then looked at me dazedly, his mouth drifting open. I pressed a finger to my lips. Mama leaned down and spoke into Sam's ear.

"Baby, baby . . . ," she whispered. "We taking you back."

Sam blinked at me.

I winked and said, "A vacation."

Mama finished unhooking Sam. I stood by the door to keep watch while Mama removed the half-full dialysate bag from the machine. She checked around the shadowy space and craned her neck back at me.

"Dialysate bags ain't in here. Can you go find them?"

I rubbed my face with my hands. "Why?"

"Go get them. Find them," Mama whispered sharply.

"Okay."

"And *shush!*"

"Mama . . . ," I said but stopped myself. I turned and left the room.

Mama couldn't argue; we had very little time and Sam needed those boxes to live. Still, White Nurse wasn't up yet. My stamping around the house certainly increased my chances of waking her. I went down the length of the hallway, slowing my steps as I reached the living room again. I crossed her shag carpet and maneuvered my way around her brown leather sofa. I found a closet in the opposite hallway, dangerously close to White Nurse's room. Where else would she stack all of those boxes?

I held my breath as I reached for the doorknob. I could hear the nurse snoring loud.

My hand slid off the knob and I gripped it again. I opened the door in short intervals until it was wide open. I scanned the space up and down; no cardboard boxes. Nothing medical at all. Just Charmin twelve-packs, foil-wrapped Easter ornaments, and shampoo bottles.

I wiped my face. I could hear Sam talking to Mama. If I could hear them from the closet on the other side of the living room, White Nurse might pick up on them talking too. Or, at the very least, she'd hear me moving her stuff around.

I stood up and turned back to Sam's room. Where else was I supposed to look? We didn't have much time left and anything could happen. White Nurse could get up; some neighbor could call the cops after seeing our van. Sam wouldn't be able to get by without the dialysis solution and it wasn't the sort of thing someone buys in Walgreens. The dialysis machines and solutions all needed doctor's prescriptions. We couldn't afford to get anything used online and wouldn't be able to get help from Mama's sister until we got to Jacksonville.

Mama emerged from Sam's room, my little brother in her arms. We stared at each other across opposite ends of the living room. Sam looked dreamily at me, his head bobbing up and down. He rested his head against Mama's neck. She bit her lips and stroked his pajamaed shoulder with one finger. I wet my lips. Could I still run?

Mama's eyes ripped back to me.

"You find them?" she whispered. "I turned off the

machine and put all the other things Sam needs in bags. Ima need you to get the machine and them bags for me. Where are the boxes?"

I lifted my empty hands. "Mama," I mouthed. "Does it *look* like I found the boxes?"

Mama stepped forward. Her face looked dirty; her shirt-sleeves frayed. I could see the gray hair sprouting limply from behind her ears. Sam clutched her collar.

"Girl," she hissed. "Find the boxes now. Find them *fast*."

I squeezed my eyes shut and opened them. My brain wanted to shut off, ankles wanted to snap.

"What do I do?"

White Nurse's door slammed open. Mama and I froze. Ice and flames and fear burned up my thighs and spread across the bones in my chest.

Mama opened her mouth, but White Nurse boldly entered the living room. The sixty-something nurse with pinched-in hips, pebble-small eyes, and a delicate coat of blond facial hair spread her legs apart on the floor. She tore off her hair bonnet and rushed over to the phone on the lamp table. She raised the receiver to her ear and pointed a finger at Mama.

"You broke into my house, Phoenix. You broke in! After everything . . ."

Mama punched her free fist at me. "Claudia! Take care of her!" she yelled. Mama held my brother close to her, then dashed into his room. Sam was crying, "Mama, hey, hey?"

Mama was gone. I walked up to White Nurse, put my hands up.

"Ma'am, we don't want to harm you. Just want Sam back . . . ," I said. She ignored me, kept yammering away on the phone. I tried to snatch the receiver from her hand, but she pushed me in the chest. I took a step back, composed myself, then tried a fast swipe at the phone, so fast White Nurse tripped and went down. She caught herself on the floor with one hand, was still clutching the phone. A male voice on the other line said, "Ma'am? Repeat what you said . . . ?"

White Nurse was on her knees, her spectacles on the thick carpet, her brown-gray hair clumped against her scalp. I knew what Mama meant when she said "Take care of her!" I'd never hit anyone in my life, never raised my hand to any girl or lady or man or boy. White Nurse grabbed her glasses from the ground and looked at me wildly, like I was something fang-toothed, animal.

"Claudia! You're the good one. Remember that!"

She was right. I was good. I was young. I liked to study. I had a future. I loved my mama. I could still be good. I loved my mama.

White Nurse wrenched her lips down. Her eyes changed colors, the hazel got blue, the blue got shit-brown, the shit-brown turned gray. Her eyes said, "Trash. She's just another one of them . . ."

"Claudia!" Mama shouted from the other room.

White Nurse said, "If I have to send you to jail I will, Claudia. You and your mother. You're making your choice."

The nurse brought the phone to her ear. I grasped the lamp and smashed it across her head. She crumbled to the carpet, stomach first. Dark blood spread from her scalp in the shape of an amaryllis. One arm was crooked, the other out, the index finger twitching. White Nurse coughed, closed her weird White Nurse eyes. Her eyes half opened, closed again. I couldn't tell if she was dead, or would die.

Mama ran in from Sam's room with three full bags in her left hand; she supported Sam with her right hand. She fell back a step when she saw White Nurse. Sam screamed and Mama slapped a hand over his mouth.

"She dead?" Mama said, returning to my side. She appraised White Nurse's body quickly. Mama's face didn't reflect a particular feeling.

"You kill her, Claudia?"

I couldn't move. My shoes felt too heavy for the floor. My hands still clutched the lamp. The shade had fallen off and was half covering White Nurse's ass.

This woman was bleeding because of me.

"Hey. Get the dialysis machine," Mama said. "I'm taking Sam to the van. We'll have to figure something out with the dialysate boxes. I got the half a bag in his room we can use when we get to Morgantown. Might not be enough, but he won't die. He'll be okay. Don't have a choice."

Mama's voice got soft, smooth. She came up to me, her arms still full of Sam and stolen things. She rubbed her cheek against mine to give me some comfort. She cooed to me like I was her baby, some mewling little child. She said, "You gonna be all right, my sweet baby. It'll be all right. This is a good thing. You doing good by our family. Once we get to

Jacksonville, we'll have a home. There'll just be family and softness."

Tears burned my eye-rims. I didn't know what I wanted to cry about. I just knew I wanted to cry. I stood back up and dropped the lamp. On the floor, White Nurse moaned.

I had to go. I had to go and do this thing for Mama. Things would be better in Jacksonville. Yes, yes, yes. I would start school again at UNF; I liked their communications program. On weekends, I could take Sam to a little drive-in I'd found near campus. Mama would be happier in a warm place, she never liked Pittsburgh winters.

Yesyesyes. Things would smooth over. Yesyesyesyes.

I left White Nurse, left her blood and funny arm shapes. I left her and went to Sam's room and picked up his dialysis machine. It wasn't as heavy as I thought. I staggered out of the room, checked the wall clock: 5:38. I followed Mama out of the house and to our van across the street. A teal Impreza pulled out of a driveway a few houses down. The car approached us slowly. I could see the outline of a man's jaw and tie knot, could see him leaning forward in his seat. Checking out the two cheaply dressed Black women carrying Miss Carson's foster child to a minivan.

Yesyesyes, things were difficult now, but we'd get to Jacksonville. We would. Once we got to Florida all would be well. It was a long drive, but we'd get out. Mama was too kind, my mama, ah she was too loving. She just kept loving everyone whether they deserved it or not. She'd taken good care of Sam, hadn't she? Mama just wanted to start over again.

Get a fresh start. I didn't need one, but she did. Ah, and I loved her. She was my mama, who gave me everything. So yesyesyesyes, I would start again, freshly with her.

The white-hot delirium of these thoughts filled my eyes; I could barely see the other side of the street, the trunk of our GMC. The Impreza passed us. See there you go, I thought. Just passed us by. God will provide, as the church ladies said.

I don't remember getting in the front seat of the car, but I ended up there, with my seat belt on tight. I don't remember pressing the gas pedal, but I did. I don't remember speeding out of the suburbs, out of Aliquippa, but I'm sure I drove faster than I'd ever driven in my life. I don't remember getting back on I-376, but I did.

I didn't hear Mama hollering until the minivan had been on the highway for a few minutes. Her voice rushed in like I'd jacked up the volume to a radio song. Mama was slapping the window on the passenger's side and saying, "You can't drive like that! *You can't drive!*"

I bit my front teeth hard. I rammed my foot on the brake and Mama nearly smashed her head on the dashboard.

"Claudia! Hurts!" Sam said.

I grunted and threw my head back against the driver's seat. I didn't want to hurt Sam. Maybe I wanted to hurt Mama, just a little bit.

"You can't drive like that with Sam in the car!" Mama raised her hand to punch me in the arm but retracted her fist. "He'll get sick!"

A police car crept up on my right side. I was too exhausted

to panic. The car sped ahead of us and exited at the Robinson Mall.

"Sam is already sick," I said, my jaw feeling too tight. The water I'd drank that morning sloshed around in my stomach. I wanted to vomit it all up. "He's already not going to make it. We only have half of one dialysate bag, Mama. You know that. What's the point of having the machine if we don't have the solution?"

Mama turned on the heat in the van. "He'll be fine. He can get by tonight on one bag."

"It's not one full bag, Mama. You saw it. It's half a bag. How are we gonna get other bags? Where are we gonna get the bags?" I said, my voice rising. "There's nowhere you can get them!"

"Danni's friend, the one in Morgantown we gonna meet, she know people who have renal failure," Mama said. She took out her phone and started pressing buttons I couldn't see. "I'm texting her now. She told me they have prescriptions. We'll be fine."

I wondered if it was possible to love Mama so much that I hated her. "Why would they share it with you, Mama? Why are you texting Danni right now? Sending out phone signals? This isn't going to work."

"We'll be fine," Mama repeated, her voice shrinking small. She stopped texting and put the phone on her lap. I wanted to reach over and snatch it, but my hands wouldn't move off the wheel. I chewed on my tongue, gripped the wheel until my palms ached.

"I might have killed that woman," I said weakly. "I might have killed someone today."

When I said "that woman," White Nurse's pink, flapping mouth and twisted arms flashed in front of me. The water rose up to my throat.

Mama leaned her head against the glass. "Don't worry. She ain't dead. I've seen a dead woman, and she ain't dead. They'll fix her."

I swallowed vomit back down and turned to look at my mother. Her face seemed abnormally wet, her eyes red-veined.

The sun budged up from behind clusters of beech and blue evergreens. That sun felt new, awful; that sun smeared violet and gray threads of cloud across the pink sky.

In the back seat, Sam sang, "Heyyyy." Mama and I looked back to check on him. His eyes were half-closed; his chin brushed his heaving chest.

"Sam . . ." I said.

"Stomach hurt. Want to sleep," Sam said.

"Okay, baby," Mama said. She reached behind her and squeezed his pudgy knee. "You're with family, the real kind. You're safe. Claudia, you need to learn to keep this thing straight. You can't drive like this, you're going to hurt us."

I flicked my eyes at Mama. My hands shook fierce. "I might be a murderer." I hadn't had sex yet, I'd only gotten great marks in class, but now I might have killed a woman. The only place I'd been outside of Pittsburgh was Akron for my softball games. And now—

I felt Mama looking at me, my voice was open and shrieking, but I didn't hear it myself.

"Are you hearing anything? You didn't kill her."

We weren't on mountains, but the blue roads seemed to dip down and jut up high. The GMC swung over the yellow line, then back over it again. I tried to right the van, but my vision flickered in and out. "I might have. You don't know everything. You don't know a lot about things, even basic things. Her name wasn't White Nurse. It was Marguerite. We talked to her at visitation. She brought us those cream cakes."

"So what," Mama said. She reached into her purse and pulled out a stick of gum. She popped it in her mouth and smacked loud. The sound was maddening.

I shut my eyes, opened them. The car swayed right and left. Mama gripped the handle on the passenger door. She started to rebuke me, but I waved a hand.

"Why didn't you just do it? Why make me do it?"

"Jesus!" Mama sucked her teeth. "I had to hold Sam."

"I could have held Sam," I said. My voice didn't sound like my voice. I didn't recognize the zigzaggy music in my mouth. I didn't like it. "You could have held the dialysis machine."

I looked at my mother again. Mama pulled a string of gum out of her mouth, twirled it on her finger. The sunrise was hurling itself against her huge cheeks, lighting up her face with new blinding color. That new face terrified me. "Claudia," Mama said. "I had to protect your little brother, just in case. He's very small."

"Mama," I wheezed. "She's still on the carpet. I'm really scared."

"You're overreacting."

"Mama. Mama!" The water lurched in my stomach. "I'm going to throw up."

"You should have eaten those sandwiches," Mama said. "I told you. You have to eat, keeps the stomach calm. I spent all night making them too. You want one now?"

"Why didn't you hit her? *Why didn't you hit her?*"

"She's a bad woman," Mama said after I was done yelling, her voice too steady. Like gray-bellied clouds before their stomachs split. "She did terrible things to Sam. I didn't need Danni to tell me that, I already knew. But I was happy she saw it, so I knew for sure. She hurt him, more than I ever could. Sure as hell, I didn't want to hit her, 'cause I would have torn her neck out on the spot."

I didn't know how to respond to my mother. Or believe her. She just sat there popping gum, calmly looking forward at the dark streets as if I were taking her to a doctor's appointment.

Mama was talking to Sam: "Sam? Wake up! Tell Claudia how White Nurse treats you. Tell her the things you don't like."

"Gonna throw up too," Sam said.

Mama smacked her window. "Neither of you are gonna throw up. Your sister just need to drive like a human being! Sam. Just tell her once, baby. What you told me when I unhooked you."

"I want to sleep in a bed soon, my-my eyes are still tired," Sam squeaked. "Miss Marguerite was gonna get a Christmas tree tomorrow. Will you get me a tree tomorrow?"

"Mama. Stop. Stop. Stop . . . ," I said.

"I'll get you a tree and a train set and a big plastic car to drive around, if you answer me . . . ," Mama said. "What didn't you like 'bout Miss Marguerite?"

My head rolled back to gaze upon my brother's beautiful face again. His eyelids were drifting down; he was clutching the gray upholstery. My brother had been pricked, opened up, and cut. His insides were always throbbing or pulsing or ripping or tossing. Sam was always in pain.

"Oh, she-she hit me," Sam said. "Lot. Like when Parkah did. On-on my nose. On-on my small parts, when I told her not to, and that hurt worst. But-but Miss Marguerite gave me trucks and boats. Only hit me when she was drinking juices, but-but then she give me toys."

"We'll get you toys. A tree. No hitting too." Mama breathed out and closed her eyes. "Thank you, Sam."

"Monster trucks?" Sam said softly.

"Anything for you, baby," Mama said.

I forced another wave of warm vomit back down my throat. Nothing mattered, made sense, everything was painful and wrong. I wished Sam hadn't responded; I didn't want to think about anything complicated right now. I should have felt better about knocking White Nurse out after knowing what she'd done to Sam, but I didn't, I just felt bad for my brother. I wished I'd bashed Parker over the head too when I'd had a chance, wished Mama were clear-minded, wished I could have spent more time at home with my brother. I wished we had more money and my father moved back to Pittsburgh to save us and Mama hadn't chosen Martin and Parker and worked so long, so my brother hadn't ended up with White Nurse. I wished I hadn't been so tricked by my love for Mama and guilt to go through with this plan. I kept wishing for things that hadn't happened, and wouldn't happen, and a big green cloud pushed against the walls of my head and tried to crack open my skull. If we were caught, no matter what, we'd be at fault, even though we weren't the only criminals.

"We have half a dialysate bag for Sam," I said to Mama. "Half."

"Good," Mama said.

"The dialysis machine is owned by the state, Mama. Where would we get bags?"

"We went over this. They have it off the market in Florida, I looked it up," Mama said angrily. She threw her purse to the floor and whipped her head at me. "What's with this attitude? You know the truth. You're not going to defend your brother?"

I focused on the road.

Mama went on, "So what's your solution, angel-girl? Don't have one. You know what I did? I made my own law: I got my son."

"Mama . . ."

"Who is going to believe us if we tell them what White Nurse did to Sam?" Mama said. "You know what e'erbody been thinkin' since day one. They already got their thoughts. Folks who tried to help us ain't got far. At best, they gonna take my boy away from White Nurse. Then give him to somebody who just as bad as me, but with a better-looking face."

My body felt light. I could barely hear Mama; peace was coming back to me again. I straightened the van easily. The sick feelings disappeared. I'd committed assault, maybe attempted murder. We'd stolen Sam, who was no longer Mama's or mine, the boy belonged to the state.

"Mama," I said gently. "You're right."

"Of course I am," Mama said. Her bun wasn't as tight as before, the hair was coming undone. Her eyes were huge, delirious.

I smiled. "Somebody probably got our license plate. The phone was off the hook when I hit her."

"Keep driving. Stop worrying. Jesus says: 'Do not worry.'"

I kept smiling. I didn't say anything because I got it. I knew. Once I knew, it was easy to toss worry aside.

Worry slid warm from my head to my hands; worry made my short fingertips glow. Worry died in my fingernails.

Because I knew, always knew. Jacksonville was Mama's land of milk and honey, not mine or Sam's. We would never enter Mama's Canaan, not one of us. We were already owned.

A cop car pulled us over at a toll station off of I-79 South. Our van got soaked in blue and red light.

The balding, egg-colored officer took our driver's licenses and ran Mama's plate through the system. Another police car appeared shortly, five minutes afterward. Mama started packing up her purse; she told Sam to grab a wrapped sandwich and the sweater she'd brought for him. She told me to pack up too and mouthed "Got to run." She said, "I'm gonna need you to follow me. I'm gonna need you to watch my back. If you have to fight them, fight them. We gonna be fine."

I sat on my hands and hung my head.

The policeman returned and asked me questions about Sam, about the dialysis boxes, about Mama. I lied, kept lying. I kept lying until my tongue hurt, until the policeman asked Mama and me to step out of the van. I got out first; Mama fell out after me. She yanked open the back door and grabbed my little brother. She flung him over her shoulder and took off. Sam yelled out, for me or for someone else, I couldn't hear. I didn't say anything back. I watched Mama slide down the sun-whitened grasses to a dark dune below. I saw her trip, catch herself. I heard Sam call out again, heard him shriek my name clearly. When I didn't respond, Sam called out "Mama!" because he didn't know who else to call.

I watched the second policeman go after Mama. He was a fit man with back muscles rippling and shifting underneath his tawny uniform. I watched him catch my mother. The first policeman slammed me against the van, rubbed his hands down my Black shoulders, my big Black hips, my Black thighs. We wouldn't make the five o'clock news this late, but we'd make the 11:00 p.m. spot.

The policeman opened his mouth and barked some question. I didn't answer. He kept yelling and his voice turned into the sound of nothing. I leaned my head against the cold, dirt-smudged window and breathed out a new kind of love for Mama. That love didn't have words, wasn't for her anymore. Maybe it was a question, something like: "Surrender?"

When Trying to Return Home

NOW THAT ANDRA HAS MOVED TO SOUTH FLORIDA, she has become Andra, Black and Something Else. In the northern city, where she grew up, they called her *heyyy, you.* In the Midwest, where she lived with her father after her parents divorced, she was Kal's Baby. In Puerto Rico, where she watched her mami pass in Ponce, Andra was la negrita, la hija de Nadia. This month, Andra has come to South Florida for a position at the marketing firm, and her coworkers ask about the Something Else. Or properly: where she is from. When she says the northern city, they say, *No, I mean . . . really?* So she tells them she's Black. Specifically, her daddy is Black American; her mami Caguas-born, mixed with several Somethings Elses. Her coworkers get dull-eyed hearing this; they are satisfied. She's bored too. This is a new thing, though, to have a boring conversation about race where no-body cares about her answers. In this Florida city, she is like everyone, bubbling with somebody else's language. Body-full with misted ancestors, yearning for old ghosts.

In her second month in the city, Andra has gotten along fine. The September wind is variously mild. She is afraid of the new rain, how it slams and sticks. Her coworkers tell her Florida weather is like this; the rains look hurricane-strong, but they'll abate soon enough. She learns how to drive better in storms. She is no longer scared. The rains let up soon enough.

Andra has gotten along just fine. She finds friends from all over the city who speak slanty Spanish like her mami did before she died. She's found friends from many countries, and they take her shopping at flea markets, bring her mangos plucked from backyard glens. They eat ropa vieja at circle tables and laugh and laugh. Andra can finally relax; her shoulders stay sweet. She considers these the kindest months of her life.

Andra has gotten along fine, but she wonders about the Something Else her friends ask about. If it's something she's missing.

One morning, in her third month in the Florida city, Andra stops at a panadería on SSW 137th. In the parking lot, a trigueña with high-piled hair looks at her twice. She resembles Andra's dead mother, mostly in the face. This woman has plate-round eyes, a short nose, ruddy cheeks. The heavy rains have made her hair shine and frizz. A red shirt hangs loosely off of her small frame. Her cart is full of pan wrapped in paper sleeves and cans of Goya lentejas, like Andra's mami used to buy. The woman sees Andra and her eyes glitter. The trigueña must have felt the crackle of recognition too. She asks where Andra is from, decides Andra's skin speaks Spanish. "Discúlpame, mi amor," she says, politely, stopping her cart. "Eres Latina?"

Andra's chest twists tight and her breaths get loud. The woman goes on about how her Chevy broke down last week after some asshole rear-ended it. Now the trigueña has to ride the damn bus, an hour longer than her regular commute. The woman repeats *mi amor* to catch Andra's attention, and this little bit of softness chokes Andra's insides. *Mi amor*, on the island, is glibly affectionate, doesn't connote anything too close. When Mami called Andra *mi amor*, Andra would imagine a heart drawn around cursive scrawl, like a valentine. That little heart would pop off her mother's tongue, sail to Andra. In her mami's mouth, *mi amor* was a promise, a forever-bond. This woman was just saying hello.

The trigueña goes on, in English, "I'm sorry. You can't understand me. You are Haitian?"

Andra is not Haitian. She understands everything the woman is saying, but she is too afraid to speak Spanish, now. She could tell the woman that she was not born by ocean rims or white-scuffed waves. Nor beside people who speak this blue city's itchy talk. She wonders what it would be like to tell this woman how lovely it is to be in a crowd where nobody remembers her skin. That she misses her mami every day and draws pictures of her mother's face in her sketchbook to make her appear. That when Andra saw her mami, days from death, on that folding bed in Ponce, Mami was out of breath. That night, Mami'd said in labored Spanish, "I don't know how to tell you. How sad it will be to stop seeing your face." How Andra said nothing then too. Because she couldn't express heartbreak in any language.

This woman doesn't care about these things. Andra rolls through the customary story about her family in Spanglish, tries to tell her about the bus line.

The woman says, brightly, "A lo menos eres Latina."

Andra says, awkwardly, "At least."

The woman says in English, "You should speak Spanish to me. The kids your age stuff Spanish in their bellies but leave it there. They eat it up but shit it out."

Andra wants to respond to this, but she freezes. She points limply to the street behind her, says clumsily, in English, the number of the bus that goes downtown. Comes in a few hours, Andra reminds her. The woman looks disappointed. Andra knows why the woman is frowning.

The woman laughs in no language.

Andra could tell her the history of her family gods. Say that her family gods are rainforest-hot, cropland-warm, dark and blazing with every-colored skin. Their mouths sound like all kinds of countries. She could tell her those gods lived wild and holy in her, in white and blue cities where her skin is remembered or forgotten, in cities where she was always one thing, or from anywhere.

But that would be boring. The trigueña merely wanted

some help, perhaps the quick entertainment of wondering if this negra was from her country, which was Costa Rica apparently, not Puerto Rico. The Florida sun slams through a snatch of cloud and catches the woman's face. The trigueña looks nothing like her mother. Andra's mami was tall; this woman is tiny. Andra's mami avoided strangers.

The woman starts toward the bus stop. Andra doesn't want her to go. Andra wants to push the woman's bread cart and ride the bus with her downtown and take her groceries up to her apartment by the shuffling shore. Andra could clean her floors while the woman takes a nap. Andra would speak shit-Spanish, cook the woman shit-arroz con gandules. They'd eat together, then sit side by side on the love seat at sunset; they'd try to find a good channel on television. They'd guess *Jeopardy!* answers before the evening dramas came on.

Andra opens her mouth to say something else, but the not-mother is gone. Andra doesn't have the language to tell her another thing. In this moment, when the woman came up thinking Andra belonged to her? They were together. At least.

The Missing One

MAMA DIDN'T MEAN TO TELL ME THIS SIDEWALK sitter—we called him Bags—was my half brother. Bags showed up on our block some Monday in March of '56, the same month Mama slipped the truth. Same year the city allowed me to attend sixth grade at Carson Junior—the white school on Delmar. Bags came to town slinging these two fat sacks, tall as a ten-year-old. He sat down, spread-legged, in front of my bus stop. Then he kept on sitting. He'd spend all day crouching or squatting or crossing his twiggy legs on gravel. Sometimes, he'd get up and scratch the sidewalk with the stub of chalk he carried around. He'd draw circles around himself, or he'd get up and shiver his hip bones to nobody in particular. None of us knew why Bags was at the stop, or who he was, really. We did know he was dirty, sooty, and loud, and our elders called him Bad. At the very least, he was a warning: Act up and you might turn out like That Bags. That Badman. That nigger. Apparently, this Badman was also my blood.

The night the secret fell out, Mama didn't want to talk about Mr. Bags. She was asking my older sister about Important Things, like how to fix a life. Hers, specifically. Every Tuesday night my thirty-year-old sister, Eppie, and my mama had "Fancy Drinks Night" or, properly, "Mama Gets Sloppy and Eppie Cleans It Up Time." I hated Tuesdays. When Fancy Drinks Night came around, I'd spend the evening reading Blondie comics in Katz's, or looking for my pal Teekie, who had a new Wibbler we'd wobble on, or I'd stay too long in Eat Shop and chew on El Diablo cigarillos right in front of the shopkeep from North Taylor. Anything to delay my going home. The last thing I wanted to do was walk in on the same scene: Eppie smoothing my mother's plaits and cooing, "You're good, baby, Mama," while Mama drank and shouted at the walls. My daddy worked on the railroads in Cross County, Arkansas, was always gone, and he'd send some money to us when he was away. He was starting to feel like some phantom, though, like the hazy outline of a man who laughed deep belly laughs but didn't exist and maybe never had. Mama suspected, since he was gone for longer periods in Cross, that he had some new girl. While nobody could prove it, Mama was always going on about it, so maybe she was right. Still, she lived in a constant state of waiting and working, of never having enough cash to take care of me and my brother Abbot, called Googs. So she'd drink hard. Eppie would bring over wine, and it all went worse.

On those nights, Eppie would see me sneak in, me: who looked so much like my father, black eyes, sloping brow, sucked-in cheeks. She'd kiss Mama's forehead and tell her, "Look, here's Kal. Our little boy star. Kal, talk about Carson, what you're learning . . . ," and then I'd spit some lie about how happy I was at that wretched school, and I'd say I learned some math equation that didn't exist, and Eppie would know I was lying, but the mood would shift for the better, quickly. I'd tell Mama life was wonderful, and I was making friends, and everybody loved me. Mama would give her hands to the ceiling, say, "Lord, my dear God, thank you for this kind news, at least you know my hopes and heart." Sometimes when I came home, Mama would be halfway through the bottle, and she'd give me cash bound by a rubber band. "This for my love, my dear Kal. Buy what you'd like," she'd say, smiling. Or she'd go: "This is for a telescope so you can see the constellations." Sometimes, she'd make me come back on Fancy Drinks Nights and ask me to read for her. I didn't know what to read, so I'd find something in the library I didn't understand like Descartes, and I'd struggle through the words while she and Eppie finished another bottle. They'd ask me about my science books too, so I'd talk about the particle density on Saturn and the Cassini Division, and they would ooh and aww. Sometimes, I would do long division on a sheet of paper and come up with the answer on

the spot, and everybody would clap, like I was a college professor finishing his final lecture. Seeing me talk about these
supposed school subjects calmed down Mama, and a calm
Mama made Eppie happy. I hated the whole charade.

I refused to tell Eppie and Mama the truth: the schoolkids
gave me hell and the teachers didn't bother to protect me.
The children at Carson saw me the way their parents did:
as a Black, little-boy symbol of the changing times. After
the *Brown vs. Board of Education* ruling, St. Louis legislators
had passed desegregation laws saying Black and white kids
had to attend the schools closest to their homes. Negro kids
were given the option of transferring from a Black school to a
white one, as long as the white school was nearby. Mama and
Eppie forced me to transfer to Carson for junior high. I didn't
have a choice. I was one of two Black children in the school
that came in that year, and the other one—a shy, pimply girl
named Bee—never talked to anyone. Bee's family wasn't on
relief, mine was, and everybody knew my parents had nothing. Maybe Eppie suspected what was going on, but only my
older brother Googs knew just how unhappy I was at Carson.

On this Fancy Drinks Night, I decided to see Googs at
the Boxing Club instead of going straight home. I hadn't seen
my brother much that week and he hadn't picked me up from
Carson. When I first got to the white school, the boys would
hound me at recess, chase me behind the school dumpster
or beat me fierce behind hawberry trees. Since Lovie High,
the Negro school, got out an hour before Carson, Googs
had started riding down to Carson to fetch me. Googs was

sixteen, his body layered with massive red-brown muscles. The other boys got spooked when they saw him float across the field toward me. That week, though, Googs had started going to the Boxing Club in the afternoon, and he hadn't come to Carson once. I thought I'd go find my brother that day, maybe tell him off or plead for him to remember me.

I rode the bus past my stop where Bags slept and got off close to Googs's gym. I checked the street for patrolling church ladies but mostly saw young girls shrieking jokes and orb-bellied porters smoking outside of Shu's Hot Cuts.

I ran over to the Boxing Club and pressed my forehead against its cool window glass. Two gloved men, fawn-like and slim, were trading blows. Their muscles, slippery with sweat, tensed and strained and glowed bright when they swung. Negro men and boys of all ages were practicing on punching bags on the floor below. I looked down at my bony wrists, at my delicate fingers. I leaned my face against the window. Any one of those folks in the gym could take out my stupid bullies with one swipe. I looked up and saw the second man groaning on the floor, the first laughing and pounding his gloves together. Googs jumped in the ring to take the fallen man's spot.

I bounded over to the door and tried to get in the club but a gray man at the front desk saw me turning the knob. He got up, staggered over, and shoved his face in the glass. The man bent down, locked the door, and mouthed, "No babies." He half smiled. I watched him turn around. I wanted to tell the gray man I wasn't a baby, I was in sixth grade and the best in my arithmetic class, but I bit down my tongue because someone was shouting Googs's name. I scampered back to my place at the glass. The first Black boy took a rough swing at my Googs. Googs ducked, and the other boy caught him on the jaw. I jumped up and down, whooping my brother's name over and over. Googs tried a hit on the other boy, but he missed, and the man took Googs out with a single uppercut. My Googs went down, face-flat. He twitched, like a trout released from water. I pounded on the glass, howling *getonupgetonup!* loud enough Mr. Bags could probably hear me two bus stops over. Finally, Googs lifted his face from the ground with his forearms, but it was too late. He'd lost fast. Too fast. I felt awful for my brother and I cried out *youokay!okay?*, hoping he'd hear me. Googs climbed off the stage and stumbled around, swaying dazedly. The gray man wiped off his face, came up, and slapped the middle of his back. He shook Googs's shoulder and waved to me. Googs saw me, slit his eyes, and shook his head. He dragged his feet over to the door, unlocked it. I ran away from the window over to meet him. I swallowed burning saliva, looked up at his wounded eyes. The left side of his face was pink, fat, and tender looking. His shoulders were damp; his pits reeked of sweat, ham, and body-spices. His face was so puffed up he couldn't frown at me, but I could see his slug-fat lips trying. He said, "What?" I could have said something kind like "Hey brother!" or "You in pain?" but instead I asked him why he'd left me that week, why he chose hitting folks for fun over protecting me, and I cussed him out. Googs's eyes bulged, growing as round as china plates. He told me I was selfish as hell, and I said some nasty words that would make the church elders blush. Then, Googs swung his knuckles into my belly, and I doubled over, hitting my cheek on the way down.

I stayed on the sidewalk for a little while, watching my big brother slink back inside the Boxing Club. My body shook, hot with all kinds of pain. I lay on the cement for a little while longer, my face stinging from the fall, until I thought I heard one of the church ladies singing, "Where we are, Lord . . ." So I struggled up to my feet and staggered home.

Our family—Mama, Daddy (when he was back from the railroads), Googs, and me—lived on the second floor of a three-story brick house two blocks off of Lindell. When I opened the door to our place that night, I passed the always-half-shut door of the first-floor tenant. I stopped halfway on the staircase. Dinner smells and sounds snaked through our keyhole and into the hallway. Glass cups clicked and clanked, stout cuts of meat sizzled and brined, dishes stank and scummed in the sink, water spit from the spigot. Mama cried, "Let's pour that one up!"

I grabbed my schoolbag and dashed up to the last stair. A slender Negro woman stood underneath the arc of the doorway, a canary hat hiding her long forehead. Charcoal curls framed her long, onion-colored face. She wore a floral dress with a heavy, multilayered skirt and her wrists wilted from the weight of faux gold bracelets. I tensed my calf muscles and swallowed. Sister Annie Richards. Sister Annie was the head of the Saintly Six, a group of self-proclaimed "elite" church ladies from First Methodist. Some of the Negro churches around St. Louis were arranging demonstrations and following King's lead after he'd organized those bus boycotts in Montgomery. I'd heard First Methodist folks and the Saintly Six talking about galvanizing, for the Till boy who'd got lynched at least, but our folks never seemed to do a thing. All talk. It seemed to me that the Saintly Six were mostly invested in chastising Sixth Street families for sport. In the name of the all-loving Lord, of course.

The women of our street loved Sister Annie and admired her yellow-tinged skin. Annie was proud of her skin tone and would brush powder on her cheeks and forehead to look lighter. Rumor had it Miss Annie tried passing for years in Illinois, that she even got engaged to a nasty white man with big money, but his family found her out, cursed her, and she fled back to St. Louis. I didn't know if those stories were true, but I did know Sister Annie used to teach at Lovie High, Googs's school, and she hated the place. Even after she left, the sister spoke to most Negro children and adults as if they were beneath her, her worst pupils.

Sister Annie noticed me at the top of the staircase immediately. "Kaleb! Get off the stairs! Are you going up or down?"

I flicked my tongue over the roof of my mouth and pointed down.

She pursed her rosebud lips. "It's after seven. Why are you out so late? How was Carson? You did well today?"

I bowed my head and gazed at the shadows sticking to my shoes. I couldn't keep track of her questions, so I answered the last one. "Yes, ma'am. Learning a lot. Already did my studies for tomorrow."

"Raise your head. Make eye contact with your elders when you speak. It's common courtesy."

"Yes, ma'am." I lifted my chin and blinked. Sister Annie reached over and poked my still-red cheek, hard. I winced.

"What's that on your face?"

"Nothing," I said.

Sister Annie raised her eyebrows. "Where did you get the bruise, Kaleb?"

"Nowhere. Playing ball, ma'am."

"Playing? What were you playing? Just playing games." Sister Annie crimped her pebble-small eyes. I licked my lips and nodded again. No way I'd let her know the truth. I wondered how bad my cheek looked now, if the skin had puffed out like ugly, leavened bread. If it looked like Googs's cheek.

Sister Annie kept staring at me. Her eyes got a little dark, a little tender, then regained their sharpness.

"You said you did your studies already? Excellent. Remember: you have a good brain. Carson is your chance. Make that into many chances. Be smart. You are not soft."

I shook my head. I felt like crying all the time, right then even, and Annie was making me feel worse. Why couldn't I just be soft?

"I ain't soft," I said.

"I am not soft," Sister Annie corrected me.

"I'm not soft."

Annie pointed her chin at the door on the second floor. I

looked up at it with her. The sour wine, dust, and oily-meat smells swelled in the hallway. The stench was embarrassing, but that was still my kin. I didn't want Annie close to Mama's room.

Miss Annie went on, "I'm sure you love your parents. But do you really want to be like them? On relief. Drinking, piddling your life away?"

"Ma'am," I said, through tensed teeth. They weren't the full way she depicted them.

See, I didn't want to be like Mama or Daddy. I wanted to be myself. I did want pieces of them—Mama's undying devotion and belief that I could do something good. Daddy's ability to keep working and sweating and keeping on. I'd rather stay on this block, with my friends, than go out into a world where flushed-faced white boys came at me, just because their parents didn't like integration. I didn't care if Carson's books were a little bit better, the school floors well swept. I didn't care where Carson could take me. If Annie's world was like Carson, I didn't like her world.

Annie said to me, "I'm going to talk to your mother for a bit, so you can go off outside. But tonight, study. Then study more. Don't stay out too long."

"Yes, ma'am."

"And don't think so much about ball games," Annie said. She let the last word lean out of her mouth, like she'd circled it with a red pen.

"Yes, ma'am," I said.

Sister Annie stared at my nose for a few seconds more. She

bent her lips upward, forcing a smile. I gave her an equally trembling grin. Sister Annie pushed past me, went up the last three stairs, and knocked on my door with two knuckles. She sang, "It's me, dears! Your Sister Annie!" Eppie cried back, "Door's open! Come in, sweetheart!" Mama's voice grumbled, "Here come the rainstorm."

The sister let herself into our place and I pretended to skip back down the steps. I reached a little past the halfway point of the staircase and stopped. I looked up, waiting until I could hear the door bang shut. Why was Sister Annie here? Was she going to blather on to Mama about how I wasn't pushing myself enough? Mama was highly impressionable and cared too much about Sister Annie's opinions, even though the church ladies despised my mother. The church ladies had sniffed around our business and discovered Mama and Daddy were devil-bad at loving but oh so good at scrapping. That Daddy stayed long on the railroads because he worked hard but wanted a different life. When the fight-noises started exploding from the upper room of our house, the church ladies snapped on their pillbox traveling caps and snooped on in. The sisters spread the news of Mama and Daddy's battles— the spotting-up necks with black and blue, the flattening of noses with fists. Still, even though Mama wouldn't admit it, she talked about the sisters' skirts, their creamy skin and musical voices. Mama would trade her life to be like them, I knew, but she hated their insides. I wanted Mama to love herself, and Annie wasn't helping.

I scurried up a few more steps to a place where I could

hear Sister Annie. I lowered my buttocks to the edge of the
stairs and opened my leather schoolbag. I took out a still-cold
bottle of milk I'd bought at the grocer's and pressed it against
my stomach.

Sister Annie's voice rang out, "Why, Eppie, you look
lovely. Now, look. I brought you and your mother some tea
packets. The sisters and I, we thought you might enjoy them."

"Well, aren't we blessed to know you. Thank you, darling!" Eppie returned with some white-woman cordiality.
The sisters liked that kind of fake talk. That's why they always
preferred Eppie over my mother; Eppie learned how white
people acted and emulated them well. She also attended
church faithfully, unlike Mama.

"I'm afraid I'm in a hurry," Sister Annie continued, "I
do apologize. The Saints need help setting up the food for
the potluck. It's not hard work, but God bless them . . . they
complain. *Complain.* I just wanted to share a few things with
your mother, Eppie. Do you mind? I would love to speak
with the good woman alone but—"

"I can stay here," Eppie interrupted. Her voice was sweet
but tighter than before.

"Patricia . . ." Sister Annie was addressing my mama.
"Patricia! You look good. Your skin has paled in this weather.
The house is cleaner too, it's wonderful to have a God-fearing
daughter like Eppie, I'm sure. I would suggest . . ." I heard
the clattering of glass and Mama hiss loud. Annie said, "Well,
there you go. Like that. A family on relief should spend their
money wisely. Those other bottles, you can put them in the

trash too when you have time. You or your husband. But this is good, what you did."

"Thanks, Sister Annie," Mama coughed out. I didn't feel like peeking into our room, but I knew what Mama looked like. I imagined her in our dusty kitchen, her cheeks greased with Vaseline. Mama was probably wearing her "home-time" clothes: a robe made of disintegrating green cotton, its collar open to reveal the tops of breasts so weak they dragged to my mama's hips. Her skull was swaddled snuggly with a pink wrap since she never wore her wig at home. I was sure Sister Annie hated Mama's look right now. I wished Mama could be dressed better, because I still thought, in all her messiness, she was better than Sister Annie.

Sister Annie said, "I came to you today to discuss a bit of community business. Your Kal. We are worried, very worried about the presence of this nigger who appeared by Kal's stop. Many children get off this bus, regularly. We've been trying to get the beggar off our street for months, but his removal isn't a high priority for the police nor our pastor. Patricia, I worry about his influence. I also worry about him attacking our children. I'm sure you feel the same."

I rolled my eyes and played with the strap of my schoolbag. Sister Annie didn't even have children. Why did she care about us or Mr. Bags? Bags was harmless. All he did was laze around and draw. And why was I involved?

"Well, thanks for worrying 'bout our Kal," Mama said. "But he's smart. Why you telling me all this?"

Sister Annie sighed. "Listen, Patricia. I wanted to speak

carefully about this with you because this is important. I was hoping you might tell us a bit more about that man? Confess if you need to. Do you know what I'm talking about?"

Mama cleared her throat. A chair scratched a rough line into the floor. I stretched my neck toward the door. Mama only made throat-noises when she was ill or anxious. I wondered why she was so jittery.

"Look, sweetheart," Sister Annie said. "The Saints have been noticing some things about that man ever since he came to town. We've been hearing a few rumors from friends of Brother Abner. We kept hushed until finally Sister Esther said the issue was distracting us from our prayers and she urged me to come down and talk to you."

Mama cleared her throat again.

"The man looks exactly like you. Got the same eyes. We're wondering why . . . ," Sister Annie said.

Eppie cut Sister Annie off aggressively. "Now, Sister Annie, if you're implying some unholy things . . ."

"I understand. I apologize. I'm simply inquiring about the things I've been noticing . . ."

Mama kept swallowing roughly, over and over. She finally croaked, "No, ma'am. He ain't one of ours."

I heard a wet smacking sound. Sister Annie's lips or a woman sucking down something.

The sister said, "All right. I believe you. I believe you because I know you're a good woman deep down, Patricia. I know you know adultery is deserving of the Flames."

"Thank you, Sister Annie!" Eppie bellowed. "I thank

you greatly for the tea. I'll see you this week at Bible study, won't I?"

"Yes, yes."

Nobody said anything for a full minute. Finally, the sister said, "I'll go back to the church. I really, truly didn't mean to upset you, Eppie, nor you, Patricia. I just want to make sure our block is clean of bad influences on our children, especially Kal. Kal is a good boy and he's going to a good school now. He can't afford to get involved with itinerant niggers or their foul business. You understand?"

"Understand," Eppie said. I scampered to the bottom of the stairs. I ducked behind a communal coat rack at the end of the stairs just as Sister Annie was making her way down. I sucked in a breath, my sore abdomen revolting. The coats stank of steel, body odor, and currant. I pinched my nose to suppress a sneeze. Sister Annie paused at the end of the stairway. I smacked away a coat sleeve and crouched to the floor. Sister Annie didn't see me, and if she did, she said nothing.

I gulped down itchy air. Was Bags Mama's boy? Sister Annie's accusations pulsed loud in my head. *Badump.* If. You. Need. To. Confess. *Badoomp.* One. Of. Your. Kin. *Shadump.*

I climbed back up the stairs to catch the end of Eppie and Mama's talk. The first thing I picked up was Mama's moaning: "—And that's what I meant! Awwww, Lord! Oh Eppie! I need you, baby. Need you!"

"Mama, honey, stop it. Stop being so reckless. We've got to . . . I think we need to talk about what the sister said. Right now, you need to tell me."

"Eppie. Kal my salvation. And you: you my only, my only strength." Mama belched. Although Mama was in her fifties at that time, Eppie did seem like the older of the two. Daddy always complained Mama was too close to my older sister. He just didn't understand Mama well. He didn't understand that Mama wasn't the sort of woman with friend-making magic, she couldn't just clutch a Jane Somebody's hand and say, "You my pal, my girl." As far as I knew, Eppie was Mama's sole friend.

I was thinking the thing Eppie said next. "Mama," she started. "Be clear with me. I love you. I love you. It just sounds . . . you're making it sound like. Like that bagman . . . is your boy? Are you—"

"Oh, hell! Hell! I'll be going there."

Eppie puffed air from her nostrils. She said: "Mama. The bagman is your boy."

My mama didn't respond. After a while, she said, "You can't go telling the world now. But . . . well . . . well you know . . . yes, that's right. You're right. The thing you just said is right."

The first-floor tenant had turned on KATZ-AM 1600, and "Long Tall Sally" came on. The song was a hip-happy soundtrack to the very un-hip-happy conversation upstairs. The radio announcer laughed, "That's a great one, ain't it!" The first-floor tenant cried, "Great, great!"

Eppie said, "Did you have that boy while you were with Daddy?"

"Yes." Mama sounded torn up. "What you want me to tell you? His name is Perry."

There was a long pause. Then Eppie smacked her lips. "What else? Like how'd . . . I don't know what to ask. Like . . . what happened?"

"Chriistttt!" Mama's voice shuddered. "Don't tell another soul, not Googs, not Kal, not them ladies. Nobody . . ." I crawled as close to the kitchen door as I could and leaned my ear against its watery-green surface.

"Of course . . ."

"You're what now? Thirty-one? This mess started six years 'fore you was born. I was a young girl, barely nineteen, and I'd been married to your daddy for three years. He loved me, sometimes. One day, I'm cleaning your daddy's pants, getting 'em ready to wash so he can go back to the roads. In his pocket, I see a letter from this woman. She was writing to him, saying she thought of his body all the time and was so happy to get his letter. So I knew what he was all about and got real angry. I knew the Pastor's brother . . . Brother Abner . . . was always looking at my ass. So I thought, hey, he like me. I started batting my eyes at him, he got to charming me, and we got close. 'Fore you knew it, we went at it, and my belly swole up. I told Abner 'bout the child but he didn't believe it was his. Said it was too dark to bring home, if it was. So I went to your daddy and told him it was his baby. He didn't believe me neither, knew he hadn't touched me most of our marriage. Your daddy didn't get too mad at me though. He felt all guilty because he knew he was fooling around. Even left that gal. Maybe he convinced himself the baby was his own."

"So why didn't Daddy stay claiming that baby?"

"Well, it ain't that simple. After I had that boy, your daddy got strange. I didn't think it looked much like anybody yet, but your daddy could see things I couldn't see. Your daddy kept looking at my baby strange. He said things like, 'That kid don't got my pieces.' One day your daddy and I got into a tussle and finally he say something like, 'I shoulda kept my other gal!' Then I got sad and stupid. So I screamed back, 'I shoulda stayed with my man! Abner was good to me!' Then your daddy knew the whole story, and it was worse because he knew Abner. And he says, 'I'm gonna kill that boy. Won't make it till one.' So I got scared and called my daddy next morning. Took him up to Eldin."

"You were trying to do right."

Mama sucked in a breath. "I don't know. I didn't feel too sad when I dropped him off. That's what make it complicated, make me bad. I felt like a bag of rocks got lifted from my back. When your daddy saw that the boy was gone, he got smooth and kind again. He said he'd stay 'round and he apologized for having relations with that whore and she'd left him anyway. I said, 'Aw right,' sorry too. And things were good for a while until they got bad. That's the story. Nothing special. I'm getting another glass."

Glasses clinked, a cork popped. Eppie hummed a little "hmmmm," as if she were still processing the information. "Hey, Mama . . . I have a question."

Mama blew her nose. "Hold up . . . ," she slurred. "My nose is stuffed up. I spilled. I spilled some of this. Jesus. Eppie? Baby doll?"

"Mama . . . Am I . . . ?"

"Fine! I'll get it myself! Baby, look. You your daddy's child. If that's what you wonderin'. I kept you 'cause I wanted child-love. I was ready for it, probably needed it. The boys are your daddy's too; they were slipups, but they his. You all fine. That one, that bagman, he's my sin. Even looks like it."

"Aw, Mama."

"I don't like secrets, but I kept one. You judgin' me, like the sisters? No, please don't. Not you, Eppie. Look. Your daddy wouldn't let me call him my son. Looked like he was in good hands in Eldin. I'd snoop in once a year and he looked good. Got some schooling, friends. He always had a look for me, a look I didn't like. Too much white in the eyes. Like a blind man, like he went blind when he saw me. That look got worse when he got older, so I just stopped seeing him."

"You know why he showed up now?"

Silence rung out. I imagined Mama shaking her head. "Don't know why he look like a monkey-man now either. I ignore him, but when I snatch a glance at 'im, he's smiling, crazy-like at me. I tried to give him some money once, but he just bowed to me and stuck it back in my pocket. I don't know how to love him. He ain't no Abbot. Certainly ain't no precious Kal."

Mama sniffed, blubbered, wept again. A wineglass shattered. Eppie said, "Oh, Mama."

I glanced down at my fingers and realized my nails were pressed into the bone of my knees. I removed my hands and studied the ten pinkish half-moons imprinted on my skin.

Mama and Eppie's voices lowered until I could only hear ob-scured syllables, clipped sentences.

I reached for the railing and I eased my small body down the stairs. I got to the last step successfully, threw open the door, and leapt into a twilight storm. A white thread of light halved the spread above me; mean winds tousled the fabric of my shirt.

What did my blood look like? Mama's blood: heavy with alcohol, light with salty bitterness and wild hope. Bags's blood: thin and watery, yearning, reeking. We all shared the same blood. The block praised me, said nice things that made my heart feel feathery. Made me feel anxious too. The students at my new school expected me to fail, counted on it.

Mama and Eppie and Sister Annie believed I was special. Like Bags and I had different-colored blood. Different com-pared to what, to whom?

I thought of Bags that night, the next morning, and throughout my classes. My teacher reprimanded me in history, specifically my eyes for snatching a glance at a flailing tree outside of the window. Her eyes were yelling things like, "Why you here?" and I was thinking the same thoughts. I was studying hard to get off that block and maybe please Mama and Eppie. Still, I wondered if all that studying and hurt was worth a damn thing.

As usual, bullies greeted me at the end of the day. They kicked me in the back and passed down messages from their mamas and daddies like "Stay in your own nigger schools.

You ruinin' the full city." As usual, I landed a few punches but lacked the resolve to fight any further. I never won against the other kids anyway. The eighth graders were long limbed and quick fisted. I had inherited my daddy's fatless frame and my mama's exhaustion. I missed Googs.

I thought about Bags as I wiped the blood from my back with notebook pages. I thought about Bags's dusty face as I boarded and rode the city bus home. I knew I would pass him today; he was always squatting in that same spot. Did Bags know I was his half brother? Had he watched me all year long, just *knowing*?

The bus grunted to a stop on Sixth Street. I flexed my fingers; a film of sweat coated my palms. I stumbled off the bus and scanned the sidewalk. A Red Cross truck was pulling up to the side of the block. A tall maid with a pixie face bumped me with her hips, but I barely noticed. A group of greasy-lipped laborers loitered outside Nelly's Diner. They wore overalls begrimed with soot spots and chewed with their mouths open. A woman with a plastic wig held open the door of a ten-cent shop with her body. She blinked slowly, furiously. She raised a newspaper up to chest level, a cigarette affixed to her lower lip. The paper headline was talking about Senator Thurmond and Harry Byrd distributing some Southern Manifesto to protest the *Brown vs. Board* ruling.

Behind the woman, a shadow leaned against the brick wall of a department store. I closed my eyes, snapped them open, and lunged forward.

Bags was in his usual spot, being very Bags-like. He'd set up a plastic cup next to his two satin bags, the cup boasting about three cents. He peeled himself off the wall and crouched down to the sidewalk. From a few feet away, I watched him pull a cylinder of chalk from his pants pocket and draw an arc.

He really was foul looking, that Bags. His body seemed dipped in dust, his skin looked like clinker brick; he was skinny-fat even though I couldn't imagine he ate much. Bags's body was sucked thin, but a soft sack of belly protruded from underneath his bone-lined chest. His hair was sectioned off into sticky twists, and little flies scooted up and down his scalp. That day, Bags wore his favorite shirt: baby blue, with the sleeves torn off. His stench never bothered me, but the other boys would hold their noses when they walked by him. To me he smelled like rust and cut-open meat, something visceral and familiar.

I stood a few feet away from him, studying the naps in his hair. I watched him draw a woman; she had pretty eyes and a big yelling mouth. He'd drawn these tears all over her face that he'd drawn slashes all over. The face was drawn pretty well and closely resembled Mama. Bags transformed when he drew. His long fingers moved the chalk lovingly, his arms gleamed brown in the sunlight. After a few moments the man's eyes flicked upward and he noticed me, a shaky kid in Converse sneakers.

"Hi there," Bags smiled. He wiped his hands on his pants.

I clutched the strap of my schoolbag and mouthed, "Hi."

"You lookin' at my picture?"

I nodded.

Bags scratched his scalp, then sucked on his finger. His eyes fastened on mine. "You have a good look on your face. Maybe I should sketch it."

"Thank you," I said and gazed at his sidewalk art. "What were you drawing?"

Bags puckered his brow and glanced at the ground, as if he just remembered he'd been drawing. "Oh. I don't know."

Bags unbent his knees and stretched to his full height. He felt tower-like, taller than everybody on the street, taller than Googs and Daddy. His height wasn't comforting; it made me think Bags could do anything to me.

"You never done talked to me before, kid. Know who I am?"

I said, "Yes."

He said, "I don't mean, I mean—"

I said, "You my half brother, ain't you?"

A dark line appeared on Bags's brow. "Your mama tell you just now? That's cold."

I lowered my eyes to the floor. It was true then. "I overheard Mama and Eppie talking about you. Sister Annie got worried and suspicious."

Bags scrunched up his nose. "You ain't s'posed to talk to me. But you did."

I nodded again. Bags laughed long. I looked down until he finished. Finally Bags said, "You a boy that thinks for himself, ain't you?"

I didn't say anything. I'd never thought of my approaching Bags as a defiance to anyone. I just wanted him to confirm Mama's story and I wanted to examine his face. See if I could find myself in his features. I couldn't. Still, I was happy that Bags saw me as a boy who "thought for himself." My parents, my siblings, and the kids at my school all saw me as a soft-spoken, skinny-armed mouse. At least somebody thought I was independent.

I asked boldly, "Why don't you got a house, sir? Mama said you had schooling."

"I know what you asking," Bags told me. "I don't got a house because my life got bad and sometimes when life gets bad you have to live outside."

Bags placed one enormous palm on my head. I bristled and almost bit my tongue. I didn't get Bags at all. He was smiling small at me.

I opened my mouth to say a thing then decided against it. I changed my mind and said the thing anyway. I liked the way Bags grinned at me. His smile felt lovely, warm. I said, "You need a place. You can use my room if you want. I'll ask Mama—"

"Kid!" He raised his hand to interrupt me. "I can't go to your mama's house. You know that, if you heard them all talking. Your mama is big, but too small to embrace me, if you understand."

"You have to go somewhere. We got other people. Grandmama? Grandaddy?"

Bags leaned his head to the left. "Grandmama too sweet

to deal with my dealings. Grandaddy ain't no good. Gave me ticks. Gave me ticks that made me bad at school, good at fighting. Good at stealing shit. Riling. Only good thing that came from him was that those ticks made me fall for a girl who had ticks too and we had a baby. But that baby went dead in her belly, and then we just kept ticking along until she disappeared, and now I'm here."

"A girl left you and that's why you're here?" I asked, disappointed. I thought he had a more dramatic story. I didn't understand the part about the dead baby much.

Bags shrugged. "Well, that too. She died, after our baby did. That's a different kind of leaving. Couple weeks after it happened, I needed some people. But I didn't have no one real. Came down here on the bus from Hannibal. I was hot. Needed to put that hot on someone, so I decided to tell your mama off. I was 'bout to cross the street when a Chrysler slammed into my ass hard, so hard I done soared into the sky. Pants fell down, hands got all bloody." He slapped his hands together. "Tell you what? That was it. Ha! That was it. All I got was dirty hands and my belt loosened up. I laughed at that all day. Laughed the next day. Thought it was a sign. I kept trying to figure it out. So I just sat down, decided to figure out the sign. Then I laid down and got some good-ass sleep for the first time in a while. Didn't figure nothing out, but I was happy to rest. A brother might do that sometimes, just lay down after Life take him out."

I turned from Bags and gazed at the street of Black folks scurrying about, smelling like cocoa beans and white people's money. I didn't dislike Bags, but he felt ridiculous to me. I wanted to tell him sometimes folks aren't allowed to give up. Life doesn't let you. On some days I wished I could flee my family and Carson Middle School, but I couldn't.

"That's great, Bags," I offered lamely.

Bags wasn't offended by my answer. He scratched his nose. "Hey. Maybe you can bring me something tomorrow? Something to read, something to eat?"

I pointed to his two laden bags. "You ain't got nothing in there?"

Bags turned around and reached for the first drawstring bag. He untied the cord and stretched the mouth of the sack open. He stretched back around to face me and beckoned me to look inside his bag. I peered inside and saw feathers, scrunched-up scraps of baby cloth, pictures of a toffee-colored girl, and tattered, weeks-old newspapers.

"That ain't that heavy. Looks like it was full of rocks," I said.

"It's always heavy, brother," Bags said. "Now you look at the bottom. You like learning, that's something you might like. You probably goin' read it in school. That should make you smart."

I reached at the bottom and yanked out a hardback copy of Joseph Conrad's *The Nigger of the "Narcissus."* I opened it. The pages were holed out and filled with hundreds of conch and cowrie shells. A little happy feeling yanked my lips back into a smile. I snorted a laugh and covered my mouth to trap it back in. Bags wasn't so bad. He wasn't a thing like me and

never would be, but he was fine as he was. Bags's face softened and he patted my curls.

"Aw, you just a small kid. Get moving. Them church ladies are everywhere, they'll spot you."

I wanted to tell him I didn't care about the church folks,
but I said instead, "Yes, sir."

I was happy to see Mama and Googs were out when I arrived
home. Daddy, I suspected, was still out at the railroads and
wouldn't return until a few days later. Eppie was tending to
her own baby, Bean, on the other side of town. I unlaced
my shoes and skipped into the kitchen to wash the encrusted
blood from my back. My spirits were lifted; I danced to the
cupboard to get the towels, jigged on over to the basin on the
floor to wash my feet. I thought of a list of things I'd give to
Bags tomorrow. Things Mama didn't need or wouldn't notice
if they were missing. I darted into my room and found a
large cotton sack Eppie had sewn for me, an extra if my book
bag broke. I returned to the kitchen and cut a few slivers of
bread off of Mama's loaf, collected a handful of grapes and
grabbed two chocolate cookies and wrapped them up with a
handkerchief. I placed all of these things in Eppie's bag. Bags
probably needed to scrub his face. I ran into the bathroom
the family shared and yanked a towel from the towel rack.
I couldn't steal Daddy's shaving cream, hairbrush, or razors,
but I placed my own little pick in the bag, reasoning Bags
needed to comb his hair far more than me. Lastly, I walked

back into my room and stuffed a pen and one of my empty notebooks in the bag. I tied the two handles together and hid the sack underneath a pile of old clothes. That night, when Mama staggered home from work and asked me about my day at Carson, I said, "It was good, Mama! Real good." She beamed and said, "Least someone's good!"

The next morning, I awoke at 6:00 a.m., an hour earlier than usual. I couldn't risk anyone from my family asking about my extra bag. Mama was still wheezing away in my parents' bedroom and Googs had not returned home that night. I dressed myself, padded down the stairs, and opened the door to a lavender morning.

Our block looked lovely naked. The dusty funk of St. Louis was gone, replaced by bright air and a grinning sky. Store-faces gazed at me plaintively as I ran; little birds twitched on the tip-tops of power lines. A few early risers creaked their doors open an inch, fluttering their fingers to test the air.

My little moment of peace was interrupted by a metallic, sputtering sound. I turned to my right and noticed a Plymouth driving in the opposite direction I was headed. The car looked familiar. I slowed my pace just as the battered Plymouth rumbled up to my spot on the sidewalk.

The driver of the car reached over and rolled his window down. An oblong, buttery face appeared, the face of a man I recognized from church. His hair was hardened against his scalp with grease. A mustache resembling a bit of black froth rested above his wide lips. His nose curved downward sharply, like a hawk's beak. I cussed under my breath. This man was

Brother Richards, Sister Annie's husband, the man she forced herself to love after she'd failed at passing in Carbondale. Everybody knew Sister Annie didn't love the brother, but he kept her well-fed and under a roof. I could have felt sorry for him, but I didn't. It wasn't like Sister Annie trapped him. He only liked yellow women; he was always comparing yellow women to blacker women. He talked down to women who looked like my mama and Eppie, and he latched onto Sister Annie quick when she came back and badgered her until he got her. Then he went around telling all his friends and my daddy how lucky he was to have the lightest girl on the block, and we all thought he was full of it. Brother Richards worked at a restaurant nearby, but to keep his wife comfortable and his debt low, he took a second job as a night-shift janitor downtown. He was returning home from his night work, I guessed.

Brother Richards waved a free hand, his smile giving up too much information about his mouth. I didn't need to see the Brother's entire gumline or the extra tooth wedged between his left canine and incisor.

"Well hey there, Little Kal! Never seen you up this early. That Mama of yours been giving you troubles?"

I shook my head. I guessed by now Sister Annie had told her husband about Mama and Bags. They looked down upon me, I sensed it, felt pity for me because they believed my mama was an ungodly whore. Sure, I wasn't proud of Mama all the time, but she loved me deeply. I wouldn't betray her. I knew the sister had done all kinds of things, but we didn't know about them.

"I have to meet with my teacher early today. Get ahead. Gotta take the earliest bus."

Brother Richards cocked his head. "That so? Thought that white school would be wrong to you. But sounds like Carson's got some committed teachers. It's a fine thing you're in that school. You remember: it's a fine thing. It's a symbol of change."

"Yes, sir."

The man's gaze drifted to the extra bag pressed against my leg. "Bus is gonna take some time, now." His eyes snapped back up to me. "Want me to drive you to school? It's not too far. That way you don't gotta be schlepin' that stuff 'round."

I clutched the strings of the special bag. "No, sir. Thank you. I'm fine."

Brother Richards continued to stare at my things. I wanted him to ask me about the extra bag so I could make up an excuse about it. Brother Richards's eyes returned to me for the last time, his smile gone. "Well. I'm gonna go get my breakfast then get some sleep. You ever need anything you come by, okay? Annie and I will take care of you."

I nodded. Brother Richards's enormous smile blinded me; his teeth were like floodlights. I turned and watched his car inch past my house, through a green light, over to Sister Annie's place. Uneasiness bubbled in my stomach. I didn't know what to do with the feeling so I moved on. I hoped Bags would be in his same spot this morning. At the very least, I knew I couldn't walk around with his things for much longer.

I found Bags snoring in his same old place. He was lying on his side, looking like some wizened hound. He sniffled while he slept; his ribs protruded through a stained dinner shirt, his chest rising and falling methodically. I studied his bearded chin, the length of his angled nose. When the wind came it brushed his shoulders tenderly like the willows of a weeping tree.

"Hey, Bags. Mr. Bags. I got you some stuff."

Bags shuddered awake. He pushed himself up with one arm, the remnants of his triceps muscle tensing. He sat on his legs and scratched the bones of his chest. Bags wiped his face with one hand and faced me, brightly.

"Hey there, kid. What you say?"

"I brought you some things. You told me to."

Bags squinted, visibly confused. "What I ask you? I don't remember."

I plopped the brown bag down on the cement. Bags glanced at it for less than a second before switching his eyes back on me.

"Boy . . . that's . . . damn . . ." His thin, ash-coated fingers reached for the sack I'd prepared for him. He placed it in his lap carefully, as if the bag were an infant. Bags sorted through the items with his fingers, sniffed the food, licked the pages of the empty notebook.

"I didn't think you'd do it. You could have gotten in a lot of trouble with your mama if she'd seen you. If anybody seen you taking things from that house."

I shrugged. "You don't like my mama. Ain't takin' all of her stuff like revenge?"

Bags shrugged. "Not really. Ain't keen on revenge." He waved the notebook. "This is yours, right? Some of this stuff was yours?"

"Yeah."

He shook his head and laughed. Huge Santa laughs. Laughs that would look like spirals if you sketched them. "Well, damn, boy, you made my day. Life at the moment. Want to eat something with me?" He craned his neck to check the street clock.

I crouched down with him. "Yeah. My bus won't come for fifteen minutes. I ain't in no hurry."

Bags ripped a piece off one of the slices of bread. "They don't like you talkin' like that. Saying *ain't*. Got on me at my school, I remember."

"I don't care," I said. "I like the way I talk. I'll say *ain't* all day and still get good marks."

Bags grinned. He raised the bread to his windburned lips. He gobbled it whole; I didn't see his jaw move.

"Well, I feel great today. You know, I like you." Bags picked a stray crumb from his lips. "Whatever you do is all right. You do whatever you want, brother. You gonna be just fine."

I bowed my head, blushing. When he said "I like you" and "brother," a rush of orange-colored feelings wrapped around me like a down sweater. Bags noticed my reaction and patted my cheek affectionately.

"Hey. Thanks for the presents, kid. I'll draw you something in thanks. Won't draw a—" Bags stopped, his eyes shifting from my face to a figure behind me. An angry dimple appeared in the corner of his mouth. He shook my thin wrists and said, "Might wanna get on the bus now, brother. You 'bout to get your ass *flayed*."

I turned my head, following Bags's gaze.

I identified the biscuity blur as Sister Annie a few seconds too late. I should have guessed that Brother Richards would return home and tattle on me to his wife. Before I could dash off or hide in Nelly's Diner, the Saint materialized in front of us. Like a ghost afire, like some kind of angel of Revelation.

Sister Annie was slightly out of breath and disheveled in a Sister Annie sort of way. Her morning face still looked fairly put together. Her hair was smooth at the roots but woolly at the ends. Three buttons were missing on an elegant cream blouse, revealing the shadow of her collarbones. Her face was clean of makeup, her cheeks flushed.

"Good morning, Sister Richards," I said with cloying politeness. "Nice to—"

She seized my arm, her nails slicing little incisions into my skin. "Kaleb!" she spit. Saliva from my own name caught in my eyelashes.

"Why are you here? You shouldn't be here talking to him! What is *that*?" She gestured at the things I'd given Bags. Bags perked up and sat on his haunches. "Were you stealing from your house, Kaleb?"

"Yes, ma'am," I said. Sister Annie's eyes stretched, and

she was temporarily caught off guard by my honesty. I didn't feel like lying. I already felt small. I wouldn't be surprised if mouse fur burst through my skin at that moment. Please let the bus arrive early, I prayed but knew God wouldn't listen to a sinner. The Lord only sided with saints.

"So you're a thief now? This is what you're going to be?"

I struggled against Annie's hand on my arm, but she felt stronger than my daddy. "You want to be like that bastard on this street? Like your mama who throws out babies like the Sunday trash? The Saints and I have been putting work into you because we believe in you . . . we believe you have chances other boys don't have. But if you keep falling into the traps of the devil, the devil will trap you."

I finally broke from her grasp and stumbled back a few steps. Sister Annie's arm remained in the air, her fingers fluttering. At this point, my only desire *was* to go to school.

"I was just giving food to the poor and homeless, like Jesus say, in the Holy Word," I said softly, not knowing if Jesus ever said those words.

Sister Annie's prim nostrils widened. "Don't you dare give your elders lip. This man willingly chose to throw away his life. You want to be him, Kaleb? Some animal?" Her pale face reddened. Her eyes turned soft, then wild.

I didn't intend to give the sister lip, but I was pleased she misinterpreted my words. Bags was on his feet now and approaching Sister Annie cautiously, as if she were a bomb ready to detonate.

"Look, don't fault the child now . . ." Bags said, "I asked

him for some things. He found out I was his half brother and was just being kind to his kin. Don't Jesus say, 'Do good to all people and don't be a perfect bitch to folks you don't know'?"

I was pretty sure Jesus hadn't said those words either. Sister Annie forgot about me and advanced toward Bags fearlessly. Her neck jutted forward and she pointed a long-nailed finger at him.

"A bitch? You meant to call me a bitch. Me? Have you seen yourself? *I'm* a bitch? I care about Kaleb. Would a bitch leave her house in the middle of breakfast to save a young Negro boy from your influence? No. I've lived on this block for ten years and only two of our children have gone to college." She took a few steps forward. Her face was so scarlet I thought it might turn into a ripe tomato. "If Kaleb does well in school, he can go to a university. He can get a scholarship. Those schools can help him. That's the way. If he gives up, gets lured into easy temptations, he becomes you. If you are capable of caring about your brother at all, you'll leave him alone. You'll find some scrap of good in your good-for-nothing body."

Bags plucked eye-dust from the duct of his left eye. He puffed his chest up and yawned. "Lady . . . ," he began, "you don't know half a shit about me. You don't know nothing about this kid neither. I've seen this boy gettin' off the bus for weeks, bloodied up. You can guess what this boy goin' through. But for all y'all's fear, you should know you can't send one Negro boy to a white school and act like he makin' wreathes all day."

Sister Annie opened her mouth, closed it. She looked like she'd been caught but refused to admit it. She returned, fiercely, "A Negro boy needs strength. He needs to learn how to behave and blend."

Bags shrugged. "Those folks gonna force him to be strong, whether he like it or not. You started 'caring' 'bout this kid when he got shipped off to that school. There are other boys on this block. This one needs some kindness. Without it, you right, he goin' end up like me." Bags seemed like he wanted to end right there. Annie paused, blew hair out of her face, and stepped toward Bags.

"That's my responsibility?" Sister Annie challenged him. "To make him soft and strong? Can you do it? You've never had to do it!" she shrieked. Tears flipped into her eyes, and I felt bad for her for a bit. Maybe she was trying to take care of me, deep down. Or maybe she was just trying to take care of herself through me, especially after she got kicked out of that town for trying to pass. I didn't really care. Bags didn't say anything, just looked at the brownstone above us.

I glanced around me and noticed a small crowd had gathered around the bus stop. Sister Annie had started to yell something else, and I tried to calm her down.

"I'm fine, ma'am," I said. "Thank you for worrying about me. But I'm fine. I'll keep studying. I just felt bad for Mr. Bags and wanted to give him some things. I'm sorry for troubling you."

The sister ignored me, still preoccupied with Bags. She looked at me hot, then at Bags. For what felt like many minutes, she and Bags stared each other down. Their eyes spit off so much fire. Their kind of hate almost looked like love.

Annie flapped her hand at a phone booth a few feet away. "I'll tell *you* something. I've received a God-given message. The police will come to pick up an animal. If they'll come for anything in this neighborhood, they'll come for that. So let's see how it works. All I need is a reason, and I have plenty."

Fury surged in my chest, lapping up all of my fear and passivity. I didn't need to be wedged into Bags and Sister Annie's fight. I wasn't something to be molded by the sister. I didn't want her. I had Mama if I needed a mama. My mama wasn't perfect, but she cared about me, and I had my own spirit, not the blue-eyed man in church paintings, if I needed someone holy. I was a Negro boy who wanted to learn some things, not an integration test project, and Bags wasn't just some soulless vagabond. His name was Perry. I wasn't so stupid and impressionable I'd do things his way. My brain was mine.

All these thoughts pricked my nerves, bolstered up my courage. By the time Sister Annie finally acted against Bags, I took action myself.

Sister Annie was halfway to the pay phone when I cried out. She ignored me. I grabbed for her arm with my free hand. She saw my hand coming and slapped my fingers hard. I ran over to the phone booth, beat her to it, and threw myself over it.

"What are you doing? What in Christ's name are you doing?" she cried. I gripped the phone booth a little harder. She started hitting me on the back to loose me, but I wouldn't let go. My hands were weak and useless, but I gripped the booth for the times the white boys told me to go back to the ghetto, and I kicked my legs for the times Googs abandoned me, for the times Mama and Daddy hollered so loudly the boys on the block would say, "We ain't gonna play at your house." Annie kept punching me on the back, and I kept gripping the booth.

I saw Bags approaching us out of the corner of my eye. He called out, "Loose it, brother."

The sister screamed at my neck, "You want to be a nigger, Kaleb? Fine. Be a nothing in a house full of niggers." She finally grabbed my head, turned it around, and slapped me with her open palm so hard I saw an array of colors. Then I saw only red, and my body floated downward.

I remember blue lines, blackness, a thin fissure of light, and Bags surging forward, his eyes furious, paternal, hot. He glared at Sister Annie the way I dreamed Googs or Daddy or Mama or Eppie would look at the bullies at Carson. Like they knew my struggles and would do anything to protect me. I released a little gasp, not from pain but from a strange, ugly happiness.

That Bags placed his hands on Annie's shoulders, almost gently, then wrenched her away from me. I heard her shrieking and shrieking and saw her kicking. Her sandals flew off.

Then, my head cracked against the pavement, and I saw nothing.

When I came to, on the ground, I saw my blood streaked on the sidewalk. I saw shadows, of a Black man encircling a tiny white-looking woman like he was holding her in place or hugging her. I couldn't tell; he hadn't let go. She'd gone slack and she was crying, her body shuddering in his arms. When Bags withdrew his hands, he stared at her face, then his fingers, then me. She walked away from him and embraced herself. Bags came forward, put a hand on her shoulder, and whispered something in her ear like, "Boy can't take no more . . ." She shrugged him off, glared at me apologetically. Annie cussed Bags out again.

The 7:00 a.m. bus was almost at our stop, but a few men broke from the crowd to examine the commotion. They craned their necks, pushed stray shoulders, shuffled our way. They were seeing my blood on Sister Annie's blouse and that Bags had thrown his arms around her, and a story was coming together.

They'd soon say the pretty Sister Annie from First Methodist had been attacked by the crazy bagman. I scrambled to my feet and wanted to make it to Bags. I wanted to thank him or curse him myself; I didn't know.

Bags noticed me and left Annie to deal with herself. He saw me tottering toward him. He scampered back over to his little alley-home, scooped up my schoolbag, and returned to my side. He spit on his sleeve and wiped my face with his shirt. He shoved my bag into my arms, plucked me up by the collar, and walked me to the door of a bus I didn't realize had come.

"Go to school!" he barked, and he pushed my back. I turned to face Bags, my lips spreading open to say Important

Things, but I didn't have any good words. I didn't know how to say "goodbye forever!" to a half brother I'd just met. I just nodded. Still looking at my bus, Bags pulled out a string of beads from around his neck. He gestured with his chin to the conch at the end of the necklace. It looked the same as the shells in the middle of the holed-out Conrad book.

The bustle of the crowd forced me to stumble up the bus stairs. I paid my fee shakily, staggered over to my seat, and pressed my bruised face against the chilly glass. When the bus grumbled, Sister Annie desperately looked to the window, as if looking for me. Her eyes weren't normal Sister Annie eyes. They were lamb-soft. Not quite Mama-like, but a little so. Tired. Sorry. Yearning.

The men were rolling up their sleeves nearby her. They started talking about protecting Annie, but halfway through the talk they'd forgotten she was there. One of the men pushed her aside rougher than Bags had embraced her. A broad-bellied fellow in gray overalls reached for Bags and seized him easily. I fought the warm rising in my eyes, for the brother I just got. Who I lost so quickly.

Before the bus pulled away, I watched Bags's mouth. I watched it as the Black folks laughed at him and as Sister Annie looked at me behind a crowd of men, with those cruel-soft eyes. I watched it as the sole police officer showed up, handcuffed Bags, forced him to the ground. I watched it as the officer saw Annie and his eyes found out that the white-looking lady was just another Negro woman caught up in women-business.

I remembered Bags's mouth decades later, after I'd gotten off the block, gone to college, got the job at the firm in Boston, and met my wife.

His lips were stretched wide. His shoulders were shaking up and down, up and down. He looked like a minstrel folk, a bad man, a criminal, a scholar, a nigger, my blood. His head was down, conch necklace swinging, as he shook with that huge mouth open like someone had told him a joke he already knew. Annie was next to him, her lips wide too; she was shuddering awful.

Maybe they were laughing.

Good Guys

IT'S BEEN MONTHS AND WE'RE STILL TALKING SHIT about what happened between Vicky D and Estelle. How V.D., that cocky pendejo, got what he deserved. Tomas Victor Hernandez Dábalos III (who insisted we call him by his full name, like a fucking dick) was in the same evening class as us. We called him Vicky D, because ha ha, no, we weren't going to respect him by saying all those names. We were all in English Composition II at Miami Dade College. My boys and me were a bunch of brutos, but we were literate at least (most of us anyway), so Comp II was supposed to teach us how to improve our research skills, come up with proposals, all that shit. To be honest, we were pretty amazed we'd made it to the second level with all our talking and goings-on in English Comp I.

That semester, I was ready to finish up and transfer to FIU. I wanted to do well in my classes and show my mami I was ready to move on to a Real Life. No more bracket racing in Homestead or checking for ass on Mid-Beach. My mami and pops were already so proud I was even in these classes, paying for them myself with the money I got from the all-day shifts at my 'mano's gas station on SW Eighty-Eighth. I wanted them to stay proud. But English II was all about distractions. Estelle Romano, hands down one of the hottest girls in any of my classes (according to me and my boys), was one of them. She had this silky copper skin, lush chocolate hair, big light eyes that changed colors when she talked, all these blond freckles specking her cheeks, and this smile that made you feel like you were having a dream day, every day. You could tell from the outline of her body, she was stacked, not to be crude, even though she covered herself in these massive skirts and shawls like a bruja. She wasn't a bruja, but she wasn't no normal girl either. But I'll get to that.

Tonto-ass Vick didn't know about Estelle's not-normalness. He came in four weeks late into the semester, gave the adjunct professor, this willowy negra with her hair perpetually in this tight bun, some sob story so she'd let him in late. He told her he'd swam over from Cuba with no clothes on and his dad had drowned to death on the way, that he was still haunted and shit. That his pops's last dying wish was that he finished college. Which nobody believed because we'd literally seen Vicky partying it up in Hialeah with his very-alive pops over the summer, and we were 100 percent sure he was Boricua puro and his dad owned a hotel in Santurce, so that would've been a long-ass swim for no reason. Profe A knew he was lying too, but she let it go, which was irritating. Profe A, Andra Something, was some part Bori, I think. She seemed young like us, but we couldn't tell; she could be anywhere from her midtwenties to early forties because of her shiny skin and rock-heavy eyes. This woman couldn't be bothered with our shit; she had some primary job, and teaching us pricks was her side hustle. I tried to sympathize with her because I'm a good dude, and our class was full of rough-talking assholes. V.D. was going around trying to get us to believe he'd sweet-talked Profe A, dazzled her with his toothy smile and dollar-brand gel that made him smell like a fucking glue factory. So the first half of the semester, we had to hear him go on about how our Profe couldn't resist his charms. Which was not only gross but total bullshit. Profe A definitely hated him and sighed every time he raised his hand. But we had to hear his come-ons, shut him down when he raised his hands to tell our Profe she looked great in her pencil skirt, help our teacher out when she redirected him. I think she appreciated us; sometimes she mouthed "thank you" to us guys, I like to think it was just me, and that made us feel special. Not that we were good students. We lied to Profe all the time about why our work wasn't done, and she knew we were lying so there was this weird, silent understanding between us built on her knowing we were liars. That whole exchange became its own kind of

truth. Which was better than the elaborate roller coaster of
bullshit Vicky D was spitting. Plus, we weren't going to go
around hitting on our own teacher like some horny pigs.
'Cause we had self-respect and respected women too. We
were raised by our mamis to be Good Guys. Not see women
like objects, you know, all that.

Anyway back to Estelle because she's what made this
whole thing go down. Vicky D didn't know about Estelle's
"condition," if you could call it that. Knowing Vick's ways
and how fine and supremely unavailable Estelle was, we
knew V.D. would try to slide in and talk to her eventually.
We watched Estelle, protectively as we did our Profe, and
saw V.D.'s slow migration from the right side of the class
to the left, as he got closer and closer to our other girl. We
saw how he'd stare and wave at her while she was scribbling
notes in class and how he'd check out her ass in the chair
when she stretched her back. We'd usually try to take the
seat behind Estelle or cut him off, so she wouldn't feel un-
comfortable. But there was a point where V.D. got in early
and took the seat behind Estelle before us. He poked her in
the spine while Profe ran the proposal slides. He asked her
all these questions and shit-talked the class, and we cared
about our Profe too, who gave us all these breaks, so one
of us would tell him to shut the fuck up, and then he'd flip
us off. Profe would see it all going down and be like, "Do
you want to have that conversation outside?" I'd point to
the slide and ask Profe a question about the proposal, which
would make her happy and which brought the class back

together, most of the time. My boys wanted Profe A to see we were Good Guys, that we somewhat cared about her boring shit. Plus, we were stopping V.D. from derailing the course we'd all paid for and stopping Estelle from getting harassed. I hoped Profe A could see my efforts, that I was pretty woke for an average Dade County gato. I one time mentioned Gloria Steinem, tried to wedge it into Profe's lecture about citations. Profe A's eyebrows flew up and she smiled, and I felt awesome. I don't know who the fuck Gloria Steinem is exactly, but I heard Moms talk about her in regards to feminism, and getting Profe's approval when I threw out that name felt pretty great. So you see, I had women's backs and shit.

The cycle of Vick being all up on Estelle stopped before the big explosion. Mostly when he started aggressively missing class. He eventually came back, midsemester, got near Estelle's desk again. So us Good Guys had to step in again and rescue our girl, at the expense of having no idea how to put together an annotated bibliography. So before I go on, look, I'm not saying I'm "good." I know how that sounds. For a girl who primarily wore robes, yeah, I looked at Estelle too, que hembra. Despite all the robes and the other thing I'll get to, I promise, her face was unreal. I can't really describe that face; it just beamed. Big puckered pink lips, high cheekbones, those freckles, man. You'd have to see it. I don't know. She wasn't conventional model-pretty; her face was beautiful in a familiarly unattainable way, like she was some chick on your block who could be in movies, and you always thought, Hey, that chick on my block could be in movies if she had some fucking talent. But she didn't, and she didn't want you, and somehow that was pretty exciting. And not to be crude, again, but it was super difficult to ignore that Coke-bottle shape. And yeah, I know that because I checked her out, but yo, I stopped after the first glance. That's what makes me a Good Guy. I looked, then looked away. And plus, the functional cockblock was this enormous, and I mean *enormous*, crucifix fixed between her tetas. Like, that cross was so big it was fucking ironic. And it was heavily detailed, like Jesus's bloody face was just suffering on her chest and glaring at you, disappointed at what a shit guy you were. This Cristo was challenging you to try something with his girl. He was like, Yo, 'mano, I'm nailed to this wood for your sins and you want to check my jeva? What a move. So what I'm saying is, if Estelle were normal, and an angry dead Jesus swinging around on her neck wasn't the biggest boner-killer in human history, I'd go after her myself. But that would be assuming she was down, and normal. If I didn't have a girlfriend, which I did, and often forgot about because she was a grade-A clinger and a little guaynabicha, I'd be on Estelle for real. (Yo, before you think I'm a bad boyfriend, I liked my girl a lot. She was fine. Not *fine*, like, Damn, she *fine*, I mean, like: fine? Everything she did was, you know. Fine enough? Maybe I was a bad guy for forgetting she existed sometimes, but to me relationships fuck up the dynamics of what's right and wrong, because everybody's wrong and everybody's right all the time. But maybe I'm wrong about that. Who knows?) Anyway, I know my boys, some of whom had girlfriends too, felt the same about Estelle, secretly. About wanting her but also honoring that crucifix and her condition. And I was respectful to my abuela, who was a Pope-loving Catholic, so I wouldn't even think about messing with a chick who wore big crosses. Vick didn't care what was what. He didn't care about the crucifix—if anything, he liked the challenge. Suffice to say, we wasted massive amounts of time in Profe's class not doing the research proposal, thinking about the dynamics of the classroom and our women, and what we should and shouldn't do. How to show the world, God, Profe A, we weren't no Vicky D. No matter how we felt on the inside, we just weren't.

So then the explosion happened toward the end of the semester. You might say, Hey, why didn't we warn Vicky D about Estelle's condition? And the thing is, we weren't perfect. We wanted to see him eat it. We wanted to laugh at him when he found out. I guess we should have thought of Estelle more, but we hated Vicky D more than we loved Estelle, it's just the shit truth. So on the day Vicky D finally decided to approach Estelle, we were ready, to protect her and to laugh V.D. out of Dade for life. It was the day the second paper was due, which was a proposal *for* the research proposal (no shit), and Vicky D was waiting on the hallway steps, just swaying back and forth like a palmera waving. We asked him what he was up to and he was grinning like a shithead and made this motion like he was jacking off, and we called him a small-dicked puto cabrón motherfucker but he didn't care. We looked behind us to see Estelle, her eyes fixed forward, skirts swinging around her curves as she walked up the concrete stairs resolutely. We moved out of the way. Wanted to see what Vick was gonna do. Vicky D did a little jog up to her. I guess we should have tried to block him, retrospectively, but we didn't.

So we all ended up on the third floor, headed to class. Vicky D was talking to the back of Estelle's neck and trying this terrible mash-up of a blaccent, telenovela crooning, and J Balvin mumble-blah. Like, he was saying, "Dime, mai, I *got* to tell you. You are the most. Moosstttt. Special thing I've seen in my whole. Entire. Life. We going to class now, but the only thing I want to study is your beautiful face. Always thought that, mira . . . óyeme," He got in closer to her and she turned around, looked back at him curiously, like he was some animal at the zoo. "Like, goddamn," he went on. "You are. So special. Mami, look at me—" Then she switched her eyes away and let out a breath, but his eyes roamed her up and down. He said: "You wearing them witchy skirts, but I can tell you are *amazing* underneath. In all the right ways. I'm a good man, nena. But I had to say it. And I bet you got the best heart. The *best* heart. Perfecta, si la belleza fuera delito, yo te hubiera dado cadena perpetua. You hear me? Mami chula, mami chulaaaa, tus ojos son como las estrellas en Paris."

His game was stunningly bad, like he'd worked on it being that bad. Like he was making fun of someone being that bad, except he was that fucking horrific. He was so bad we needed a moment to figure out how to laugh because we just wouldn't believe a human being would willingly tank so abysmally, in front of us. There's shooting your shot and then blasting yourself in the dick with a Mark 2 Lancer. I was standing next to my boy Mateo, this mop-haired, nice-looking Dominican negro who grew up in New Orleans, definitely a good guy who worked at this homeless kitchen downtown and would totally tell you who Gloria Steinem was. Best guy I knew. But, listen, even Mateo was covering his mouth with his hand, his body rocking with silent laughter. I couldn't laugh myself; I just let out a loud *wow* that was meant to hit like a slap. I made sure Vicky D heard me so he knew the gravity of his failure. His eyes flicked up at us, like we wanted, but he went back to Estelle. Our reactions didn't register. He was excited about the audience, apparently.

"So—" he went on to Estelle.

"Hey, thank you. You are very sweet," Estelle said, with effort. "We should get to class, yeah? Big day!" And she turned from him. She didn't need to be that nice. Some girls were just So Nice, Too Nice. Guys were shit, I knew that, I was one of them. If I were a girl, I would have personally kneed V.D. in his baby huevos, but I ain't no girl. And I don't know the dynamics of being a chick, I ain't a psychologist. Anyway, we cried out, "Fuck you, V.D.! Leave her alone!" And we started going over to Estelle finally, to protect her, but then we didn't want her to think we were coming on to her, or were in any way associated with V.D. So we kind of just lingered there, let her keep walking to class. I threw up a thumb and mouthed "We got you!" and she looked confused and I tried to communicate that we meant we supported her, not that we *had* her, but didn't know if she understood. We didn't know our next move; we kind of just stayed there doing nothing. Didn't make a decision. Plus, we definitely wanted to see how far Vicky would go before she told him the truth.

She was halfway down the hall to the classroom. Vicky D started following her, unfazed, so we trailed him. There was a train of us at this girl's heels at this point. Vick was turning his head, looking at us for support, and we just threw him a middle finger. He thought we were egging him on, so he spun around to us (and tripped on his own pants while doing so, of course) and said, "Watch this," and he spun back around all sloppily and kept going. Vomit.

He threw a hand on Estelle's arm, and she stopped. She turned swiftly on her heel, yanked her shoulder away from him. Vicky fell a step back, ran a hand through his greasy hair. We moved off to the side and leaned on the iron railing near the classroom door. Estelle's mouth was wiggling, her eyes were crinkling. V.D. folded his arms and gave her an up and down, kept biting his lips and licking them. We made loud gagging noises.

To get to the best part. Vick was ready. All up in her personal space. His body was inches from hers, he was close as his feo face could get. She looked a little scared but also like she didn't care. Then she just started smiling and we were like, What the hell? And that smile was huge, near delirious, and for a second we didn't know what to do with that smile, like, was she interested? Just in that second, we burned with fury, this time at her. I don't know why. She hadn't really done anything wrong. Then we understood that that was all she was doing—just smiling. She looked at us then back at him, and I could see that she kind of hated us, but I wanted her to like me so I cried out, probably too desperately, "Estelle, we've got your back!" I said "we" so my boys didn't think I was abandoning them to get points from her, though it was pretty obvious I was self-involved. Mateo and a few others in our crew chimed in, "We got you!" And she ignored us, but at least she knew we were supporting her. She was looking at V.D., smiling at him, and he was smiling too, thinking she was flirting, but then we got it. She was ready to deploy the truth, viciously too. We liked her again, loved her even.

"Hey. Give me your number," he hissed. "Come on. I want to take you out."

Then, she says the thing we all knew: "I'm already with someone. But thank you, Victor."

We cried, "Victor!" And Vick, this fucking shit, who thought he could snatch anyone's girl anyway, rolls on. "I don't care. Let me know if he don't work out for you. Relationships don't last forever. True love does. I'm talking 'bout what's real. I know you're a one-of-a-kind girl. I don't say this a lot, but it's true. Believe me—I'm a picky guy. I bet that man don't treat you well all the time. I bet he ain't everything to you 24-7, is he?"

Now, this was still pretty bad, but I started wondering, since Vicky D had been with a bunch of women—albeit not the most confident girls—who does this shit work on? Why? Do they just want to fuck? I also wondered about the anatomy of this terrible game, because I'd definitely told a girl that I was a picky guy, that she was one of a kind and not like the others, when I generally thought she was like a few others but in the moment she was just the one person I was talking to. And, when I tried to steal a girl away from some prick, I'd tried to get in her head, tell her he was crap, I was better, I'd treat her best, blah blah. Like, making a girl feel like she's the only one you want, while simultaneously showing her you could get anyone, that's Game 101. Maybe it was because he was piling it on all at once that made it so fake. So if Vicky D was clearly a shitty guy, then that just meant I was a shade of shitty. Like everyone else. Or maybe I was just a normal guy, and what made me so good is that I was thinking about this shit. Anyway, tons of mierda was passing through my mind watching this face-off, and for some reason, the more I watched the more my hate grew for V.D. Like I hated him so much I wanted to tear his neck out, at that moment. I tensed my fist, imagining myself doing it, saw my hands gripping him and Estelle looking all wide-eyed at me. Would she think I was too aggressive, just some beast? Or would she think I was super macho, because I was coming in to save her?

So Estelle responded to this I'm Better Than Your Man shtick with, "I'll be okay. But thank you."

Damn right. Stay in your power, Mami. Really get up in 'em. Tell him now who you are. We started singing, Eh, Victor, eh Victor, small-dick puto, over and over again like it was a chorus, and he was bristling. Now he was basically spitting into this girl's face and whining, "You sure? You sure? Cause you ain't really seen me. You don't know who I am. If you see meeee—"

And she stepped back and touched the cross and said firmly, "I'm okay. I'm not available. I have to go to class."

Then this bitch-made nigga got to *begging*, "Oye, just take my number, Estelle. Come on. Just take it. Take my number."

She said no again, and he was, at this point, screaming, "Do it. Just do it. Come on. I'm nice. I'm a good person. I just want to be your friend. You don't want fucking friends?"

I was thinking then, Fuck my boys, I'm going in. Gonna do some talking, do some pushing. Help her out. If she had even slightly glanced my way for help, I would have bounded over there. Trust. I checked with my boys to see if they were going to do anything, and they were like me, sneakers digging into the floor, wondering if they should run in. It was weird, part of me wanted to help this girl out, the other part wanted to see Vick self-destruct epically. So then Mateo got up, looking like he was gonna come to the rescue, like a Good Dude would, and I got in position too. He glanced at me and whispered, "I want her to have her own agency. But this is too much . . . I don't know what to do . . . ," and I nodded too. I had to try that shit myself later, i.e., "I want her to have her own agency." So now I was doubly feeling insecure and thought about outrunning Mateo, because I was not gonna let Mateo, Resident Good Guy, who got both pussy and dick at equal speeds, which seemed kind of unfair to me, be the only hero.

But Estelle ignored us. Her body said she didn't want our help; she was stiff-backed and strong, her hips locked. She didn't look scared, and it turned me on. Vicky D was just bouncing up and down, confused.

Then, Estelle released the gold, the thing we all knew. "Victor, you do know I'm in the Sisters of Grace? In precandidacy. That means I'm studying to become a nun. I am a friend to everyone, but I am not available to be your friend."

We yowled. We screamed! We cried with joy. Vicky D didn't get it. He thought she was joking. He looked her up and down, glowered at J. Cristo swinging miserably around her neck, and he laughed once, hard. He came toward her again and she held a hand up to his face.

"Really," she said. "Thank you for your compliments, but I need to get to class." Ah, I don't think my belly ever ached that bad, ever, from laughing. Maybe this isn't funny to you, but it was to us: her condition. Whether you believe in whatever she was talking about, chastity and sisters and holy orders or whatever, having a nun without a habit in class who we all were attracted to, who Vicky D was trying to hook up with was just: chef's kiss. And the perfect situation for humiliating this guy we hated the most. So we clapped and hooted. Vicky D's face! Man. You had to see it. That face looked like Potato Head parts rearranging. Even Mateo was coughing, he was wheezing so bad.

Estelle tried to end this interaction and she repeated, "I'm studying to be a sister. Again. Goodbye."

"A sister? Come mierda. You look Black enough to me."

"I don't have to wear a habit for you to respect me. I'd appreciate your respect. Also: *No me jodas*."

I pumped my fist in the air. Vicky D was looking at us, then her, near helplessly, because we held each other and sang, *"No me jodas, no me jodas!"* our voices filling the hallways, and Estelle got him. Done. And he yelled, "Puta, you ain't no nun. Just take my number," and then he reached forward to grab her phone from her purse and brushed her chest in the process, and we definitely all surged forward this time, but then, this nun, our beautiful unattainable Estelle, pulled her arm back and clocked him directly in the fucking jaw. Not kidding. That little mami had a great swing, and it connected brilliantly, and when it did Vicky D did this little dance to keep upright, but he was so surprised he stumbled over his own legs and flew to the floor. We rushed up and tore out pages from our notebooks and hurled them at him. We were yelling, You comemierda que pendejo motherfucker, hijo de gran puta, Padre, Hijo, Espíritu, and while he was getting up, trying to fight us, Estelle slipped out. He scrambled to his feet, pushing us off him, looking for

Estelle, like he was up to something worse. That wasn't going to happen. We restrained him, all of my boys versus this one bitch.

V.D. tried to sock Mateo, but Mateo dodged him and got him in a headlock so he couldn't run off after Estelle to the classroom, and while he was struggling, we were laughing. He started getting tears in his eyes and threw his feet at me and my boys. He was going on, "Yo, she ain't no nun. I'm a fucking Catholic! I can tell! That ain't right! She's into me. She's into me. Did you see that turtleneck?"

Some of my other boys started blessing him, kicking his shins. He got redder and redder and he tried to land a hit on my boy Mateo but M dodged him. My other boy, this white kid named Dredge, pulled up and got V.D's torso, and we clapped. V.D. kept kicking at us with his stupid little legs and viejo-style leather shoes from like 1913. And we kept hollering at him. He tried twisting and turning and whacked us with those twiggy legs at least once. We grabbed his shirt and pulled it up and we spit on his stomach and told him wipe up our cum, and he was just swinging those baby legs back and forth. Saying he was going to get Estelle whether she liked it or not. So we spit on his stomach again. The more we yelled, the more our desire for Estelle blew from our bodies, the more our hatred for ourselves transferred over to V.D., this clear cartoon of a shit guy with his slicked-back hair and skinny body, who was still yelling about getting Estelle's pussy. The more we humiliated him, the more we felt high. We lifted from the ground, near levitated. We wouldn't be surprised if we floated over the MDC, like something omnipresent.

At this point we heard this clickety-clacking, and it was Profe A, walking in with this leather bag on her shoulder. She saw us all grouped near the classroom. She ran up quick when she saw Dredge, Mateo, and me holding V.D. in place. Dredge let V.D. go and V.D. bobbed up and down, lingering, considering whether to knock us out (he couldn't). I looked over at Profe A to make sure I could get in front, protect her if something went wrong. Profe A had no idea what was going on, and she was staring at me confused, and she mouthed, "What the hell is happening, Alejandro?" and I knew she was worried because I'd never seen her cuss in front of us. I imagined how grateful she'd be if V.D. tried to attack her and I threw myself over his blows. How I'd punch him out harder than Estelle did. How Profe would hug me and say, "You're one of a kind, Alejandro, one of the best ones . . ."

But V.D., like a coward, sprinted off, notebooks with no work in them scattering all over the hallway as he flew off campus, back into the city. Probably off to manipulate some chica to regain his manhood. I felt bad for whomever that chica was, whomever had to deal with his horrific game. Thinking about V.D. going after some lonely girl made me wonder if my moms was lonely with my pops. How she felt when Pops laid prostrate on the couch, sighing about how life would be better if this or that had happened. When he really meant he was looking for some new girl, hoping she would bring him happiness he couldn't make himself.

I wondered if Profe A ever got lonely, at night, grading all of our bad papers and wondering if she should try for a better-paying part-time job. If Estelle got lonely when she was talking to this invisible dude in the sky and wondering if he heard her.

Anyway, Profe A ran up to us, and she looked mad rabiosa, and then we told her what happened with Estelle. We told her how we protected our nun-nena. We slipped in the part about her clocking him in the face at the end so Profe heard about how great we were first. Not to take that away from Estelle, but you know. Profe A asked a thousand questions that we answered accurately and she started softening toward us and we got happy about that softening, so happy we were gonna bust. Her eyes were switching back and forth, like she kinda didn't believe us, though. So she just waved her hand for us to stop talking, told us to wait outside, and went in the classroom to find Estelle. I ran up to the room window to see what was going on, and Estelle was just sitting there looking calm and unbothered like the Baddest Bitch. Profe A was leaning down, whispering to our girl, then glaring at us, then focusing back on Estelle. After like ten minutes, Profe A came back out and said, "Okay, just get back in class. We have a lot to do today." And she looked at us Good Guys, and I'm sure she was looking at me but maybe I just wanted to remember it this way, and she said, "I'm going to make sure Victor doesn't come back. Thanks for holding him, who knows what could have happened." Then Profe turned on her little heel and bumbled back into class all purposeful and me and my boys high-fived each other. We ran into class with our chests puffed out, feeling incredible. Estelle still ignored us when we tried to catch her eye, and Profe A carried on with class as if nothing had happened. We raised our hands so much, Profe A had to tell us to calm down; we were just as joyful as you can imagine. I think that must have been the most we participated in that course, although we forgot to turn in the proposal for the research proposal that day.

V.D. was forced to drop the class, but Estelle stopped coming too, even though it was midsemester. I knew she was doing great grades-wise, so I didn't get it. When I tried to get some answers from Profe during a conference about my proposal for the proposal, she evaded every question and told me I needed to apply myself more to my paper. "You're gesturing toward self-awareness that could really make the difference, Alejandro."

I wondered if us guys had been too much for Estelle. I thought about what happened to that girl a lot, at least until the course ended. What I could have done to make her come back. The class was also less fun without the Estelle–Vicky D drama. We didn't miss Victor's presence, but we missed Estelle. Our pretty nun in the corner, scribbling away, Smiling Nicely.

I thought about Victor too. I always came back to how much I wildly hated him. Flaming, irrational, monstrous hatred. Sometimes I was afraid I looked like Victor to other people, to my jeva, to my exes and Profe. I had fantasies about going over to find him in Hialeah at some shit bar. Seeing him feeling up some girl's culo. I'd shoot him in his temples with my pops's rifle, so he didn't exist in the world anymore. For women. For me. But then, I'd feel bad just thinking about all that. I wouldn't even know what I was feeling bad about. Wouldn't even be 'cause I'd just fantasized about killing a guy. I'd just feel bad, in general. 'Cause I was trying to be good.

Mira, I thought about Estelle every night too; that was the fantasy that made me feel the worst. Made me happy too. I hoped all the other guys in the class felt the same way, so I wasn't the only one. They must have. I hope they did.

In the dark of my small dorm, I'd think about her. When my roommate was snoring loud or off banging some Kendall chick, after I'd get a call that my papi didn't have the money to help me out with the semester when I knew for sure he was just hoarding it, I'd rub one out to this Facebook picture where Estelle was wearing a sundress. Just Smiling Nicely at the sky. I'd imagined fucking this good girl to sleep, telling her to wear the habit, even though she didn't have one. I'd buy that shit from Party City and gently ask her, all gentlemanly, Put that habit on your head, and she'd say, You do it, Alejandro, and that would drive me fucking crazy, but I'd be like, No, you got to, you got to do it yourself, it's about you *having agency*, and she would throw it on and I'd rip it off, and it would fly across the room. I'd ride her so hard she'd forget everything but how good I felt inside her and she'd smile because I'd made her happy.

And she'd be smile-crying, enjoying this like it was the best thing in her life, because it was, I bet, because what I was doing to her was saving her from whatever sadness made her go into that nunnery-convent-thingy. She'd be looking me in the eye, so happy, and screaming God Jesus God Jesus God, and *God* would turn into my name, and then it would be *GOD*, and when she talked about God she would be talking about me, before she came, gloriously. So many times she and I would lose count. After I already cleaned myself up, she'd still be calling me God.

I imagined looking at that habit she threw off, seeing it strewn on the floor. While she was sleeping, I'd pick it up. I'd sit on the windowsill of my shitty apartment, holding that wilted thing. I'd feel the wet hot of the South Florida air and look through the window. I'd watch some people jauntily walk along below. I'd light a cigarette and stare at the stars and think about the immensity of the night and wonder about God out there in the wind, pissed at me for taking his girl, contemplating his next move. Would he strike me with a bolt? Drown me in a hurricane? Would my brakes go out and I'd sail over the MacArthur into the purple sea, while all the cruise ships came in? And in that moment I'd get hard again, imagining I'd done something really important. Like I was Napoleon, I don't know much about Napoleon, but I'd be like some macho who'd gotten away with Something Big. Torn out a piece of the universe. Gotten some kind of revenge on whoever fucked up our lives. Gotten assurance I was far greater than my shitty pops, who spent all his time schooling me on how to be a man while also obsessing over his bald spots and spending his nights flirting with women my age. What was more alluring than taking a girl from the Highest Competition?

But I was an Abuela-raised Catholic. Always sinning and feeling guilty. My mami told me to treat girls right. So I asked God for forgiveness, just in case, and overcompensated by being sweet to the girls in my class and to our Profe. The Estelle who said yes to me in my fantasies wasn't the Estelle from my class; she was a girl in my head, maybe some part of me.

See, J.C. gave us guys a total setup: *What comes out of a person is what defiles them*, he says. *For it is from within.* But what if you just let the thoughts come and see what the fuck happens? How else do you figure that shit out, J.C.? You meaning to tell me J.C. was thinking pure every day of his damn life? Ha! I don't believe it. That nigga was stressed AF. Total setup.

There's a difference between knowing and knowing not to be stupid. Between fucking and not being fucking stupid. Right? That's what I think. But I don't know shit.

A few months after Estelle was gone from our class for good, late one night I texted this chick I was chilling with a while back who moved to Michigan when I had nothing to do and I was alone in my apartment again. The cicadas were screaming murder that night. I told her I was sorry for some shit I don't remember I did, probably involving sexting bitches. I said, "Sorry you're so sad." And she got even more mad, so we got into it for a minute and I was like, Well, we could talk about this when you're less angry, but then I thought about how I was an asshole for stringing her along after I dropped her. I wondered if I was an asshole for calling her up out of the blue to relieve my conscience, or if I was an even better guy for apologizing to her. Anyway, as she was screaming at me, I was wondering what she was wearing, and I looked her up on Facebook and she was even more beautiful than I remembered. She looked a little bit like Estelle. And I told her halfway through her yelling that she was pretty, and she said, "Please stop," and I apologized for real. She got all soft; her energy felt like one of those cashmere sweaters the Bal Harbor chicas wear. And I got soft too. So I said everything I was thinking to my ex out loud, about how I kind of loved her, and she got quiet again. She said, "I wish you'd figured this out earlier." Then I couldn't remember why I broke up with her in the first place. I started saying sorry more, but she said gently, "Good luck, Alej, and best to your girlfriend," and hung up the phone. Then I realized, Oh shit, I do have a girlfriend. I called my jeva up and probably shouldn't have started drinking whisky when I did it, because I definitely started getting hammered. I asked my jeva if she wanted to get banana splits at Jackson's tomorrow to celebrate our anniversary, which was the day before and I'd forgotten it. She said our anniversary was last month and we'd already celebrated it at Jackson's. I said, Fuck, just kidding, let's get some splits, now, just for fun. And she was like, Good luck on your research proposal, Alej. And I was like, Shit, I still need to write that. So I told her I'd do the proposal and afterward I'd ask her some questions about the paper. See, my jeva was actually pretty smart, just like my ex, and I forgot about how smart both of these women were. So halfway through the conversation about splits, I just let loose everything I was thinking to my jeva, really unloaded. Told her about Estelle, and my ex, about wanting to please Profe, about my pops and my sad mom. I waited on the phone and didn't hear much. I was legit nervous. Then my girl said, "I think we should break up. Being with you is bad for my mental health. But you're gonna figure everything out. I believe in you." I should have gotten angrier, thought I would, but I just felt hollow. I felt ugly and real and, weirdly, brimming with sun. I could see my (now ex) girlfriend on the beach, grinning and free, not waiting on my calls all the time. I felt liberated just imagining her like that; it was even better than the Estelle fantasy. So I said something like, Hey, I'm there for you, hit me up if you need me, you know I always got you. Stuff like that, and she said, Okay, Alejandro, and hung up.

So, listen: I don't know if there's a difference between what comes out and what lives within. Between being stupid and fucking stupid.

All I know is that night, I went to my bathroom and started shaving my beard. The window was open and the thick winds made me feel self-aware. I thought, I ain't gonna be my pops, I don't need to jack off to God's girl. I could just chill, shaving, trying to figure out what kind of man I should be, alone.

Fevers

KAL HAS A REAL FEVER—THE SORT THAT SITS HOT in a head, the kind a man gets from not letting his nose faint in a pillow long enough. Kal should be in the city, in bed. Kal should be finishing the annual reports for that skinny-faced Robert Falls, but he is back again, on the South End, to see his brother and his friends. He feels old, looks it too. The men are eating chicken and chips in a green-roofed joint off of Delmar and they're making jokes about Nadia, the light-skinned Latina he's loving now. Kal isn't talking about Nadia; he's telling them he's sick. He's telling them his face feels green. The group is saying something about his fever being jungle-like. Kal isn't hearing them; he can barely see their mouths flapping and spitting stupid. Kal's neck is bobbleheading and he feels like a toy, empty and smooth in the face. They say something like, "Look at him! Girls he get, fine as fuck. Shit, man. And he's out here crying." The group is ordering something fried and fatty and their lips are slick with grease. Kal thinks, I don't have to keep coming back home. Why do I keep coming back? His fingers are shaking like they're playing invisible piano keys, but the group can't see his hands. The spaces under Kal's eyes are bruised and raw, and the men don't care. They are asking him if he thinks he got on, if he thinks he's better than them. Yeah. Uh. Huh. Ho, yeah. They are talking about his girl as if she is a radio line or a long dream or an exit sign, not a person. Kal's forehead burns the more they speak.

Kal's love for Nadia was a coincidence. That love straddled him and choked him, coated his work-worn spirit with a cooling balm. Nadia had just transferred to the firm. She'd seen him, at 9:00 p.m., at his desk with his open hand pressed against his forehead. Nadia walked over and squeezed his shoulder. She said, "Tired? I'll get coffee. My potatoes are in the break room," and he didn't look at her but thought: That's nice. Then he did look up and realized she was beautiful, but not because of her skin or because her hair was soft and light. He liked the little dimple that studded her left cheek. That she knew how to smile, showing off all of her front teeth. She was the only one in the office who could tell he was tired, when he'd worked so hard to look cool-faced.

Kal thinks about the group and the things they say now. He thinks about his Black mother slumped on the sofa with high slopes of stuffing. He thinks about her always-dry hands and wrenched-down frown.

Kal thinks about the first girl he met in college. Immediately beautiful, shining. Black with swinging braids and a mouth that tasted like raspberries. She got him. They didn't work because they didn't. She thought he was too ambitious to love anyone back then, and she was right. He had too much drive to stop for love. Kal thinks about the other girls, the Taiwanese actress who left him to learn Portuguese in Brazil, the Idahoan white girl with the nose ring and the violet lipstick, the Nigerian writer who was living in Istanbul now. Their faces blur in his head, get sewn or smeared together, like a tight stitch of lady-feelings. Any one of them could have saved him, if the conditions were right. Any one of them could put him in the ground.

He thinks about the next day. He will be in the office. Nadia will kiss him on his head when nobody is looking. She will tell Kal he is good and strong, and Robert Falls will tell him he's always missing some mark.

The group is talking and they keep talking. They say that Kal is getting a big head. That his head is growing so big, like a balloon, someday he'll just float away. Kal closes his eyes. Nobody cares that I'm sick, he thinks. They only want to know what success tastes like. It tastes like fever.

Abbot let the rest of his group walk out before him. It was February, a day with too much weather. Little hail threw fists at sleek-slick car windows. Nasty cold sat hard on all of their shoulders. The air was so mean it made them shuffle fast to Abbot's SUV. Kal was walking quicker than the others. The group was yelling jokes at his back while he leaned sideways. Kal didn't think the group was joking, so they had more fun poking at him. They ran up and punched Kal in the shoulder. They guffawed in his ear and called him a white boy who talked like a whiter boy. Kal growled and started run-walking. Abbot saw Kal coughing as he moved, saw his younger brother tearing off his hat, despite the winter chill. He knew Kal wasn't well off. Abbot knew Kal was sick and looked bad. Kal had too many bones in his face now; he was sucked of water and blood. That stuck-up piece of shit.

Abbot had known that boy forever, knew him better than anyone. They were born four years apart. Back when Kal integrated Carson Elementary in '56, Mama had asked Abbot to stop by the joint when it let out and make sure the white boys didn't kick Kal's dark ass. Abbot would leave his school early, wait outside of Carson until the bell rang, every week and most afternoons. He'd see Kal leaving Carson, see him get promptly chased into swaths of flower bushes and short trees. Abbot would see a half circle of white faces surround his brother on the playground, and Abbot would pick the boys off, one by one. He'd throw Kal's little body on his back and get to running before the teachers saw them. Abbot was the muscle, Mama said, but Kal was the bigheaded brain. Kal was smart and the whole family knew it. Mama was always asking Abbot to take Kal to after-school programs to make sure he stayed smart and did something with that big head. Abbot would take Kal to math classes at St. Sebastian; Abbot bought Kal an antique abacus, with his money, for his birthday. When Kal got older, Abbot went to Kal's football games and science competitions and let him borrow his car so he could pick up the girls he liked. Abbot went to the war and got demons clawing around in his head, and Kal went to Princeton, and now worked at a law firm, and hired a tiny Black lady who looked like Mama to clean his floors. Kal seemed high up, enough that he couldn't see the world as it really was anymore, but Abbot knew him. And here Kal was, pouting. Sick. Fuck him.

What was Kal sick from? Working? The whole family worked. The family had been working their asses off since Kal was a little boy. He was younger than his siblings; they took turns taking care of him. They didn't have time for high school studies; they were too busy busting their asses in factories, or in groceries, or in corner markets; they were trying to put all of their money in the pot. And here they all were. Moneyless, with little help from Kal. And there he was.

Let Kal get bothered by the group's white-girl talk. Kal cared too much about what they thought. He should remember that Mama worked her whole life to give him money, keep him dressed in handsome clothes. Everybody else was working when he was little, eating cheesecake. Everybody else needed money now and didn't have time to sit at home solving math problems and dreaming. Kal had that luck. Abbot was sick and dying on the inside too. He saw

Kal cough; Kal kept coughing. It was cold for everyone, not just him.

Abbot still loved Kal. It was a tired, old love. It was damn near obligatory. Sometimes, Abbot wanted to rush up to Kal and protect him from all kinds of mean winds, to punch away all of the things that made his little brother's face weary. He wanted to resume his role as Kal's protector, the person Kal needed to get on. He'd imagine himself doing that, rushing back in, all puffed up and ready to save. Abbot would have his purpose back, then. Other times, Abbot wanted Kal to start dying. To get weaker and weaker. Until Abbot had to pick him up, carry him home. Put him on Mama's couch, in their house, and all Kal could do was look at his family, moving around him, moving, moving, and he'd lie there, his eyes boy-like. He'd lie there, gloriously weak. Abbot would stand above Kal then, just watching.

I Don't Know Where I'm Bound

IT WAS MAVIS'S LAST DAY IN NASHVILLE AND SHE was ready to kick that city for good. Mavis, thick-maned, dark-hatted, and Black, looking nothing like Nashville's poster girls, was throwing back a shot at a blues joint in Printer's Alley. Her sister, Estelle, a nun turned tarot card reader turned barista, was sipping soda on Mavis's right. Skitt, Estelle's painterboy friend, flanked Mavis on her left. Those two prattled on about nothing-stuff. Mavis was just counting the hours until she could get on I-24 and ditch Tennessee for good.

Nashville was fine enough. Just another city to try then drop. Mavis felt the same way about it as she did most places and things: nothing. Starting with her parents. Mavis's father was a decently known Italian American theater director who'd written a Broadway stage play about some guy who offed himself after some girl left him. Then he got a slew of awards and proceeded to off himself a year after Mavis was born, just like his main character. Her mother was a Black Boricua actress who died from melanoma two years later, and that woman was known primarily for being "on the rise . . . ," A "singular talent" and "emerging," like she was some half-formed thing. She was mostly known for being married to Mavis's kind-of-famous father. Too young to know or care about either of these people when they passed, all Mavis knew was that they were dreary and had failed and died. And she wasn't going to live like them.

Mavis spent most of her young life in New Orleans with her mother's uncle, this Puerto Rican sax player who lived in Southern Louisiana. This guy toured the country and shuttled the twins, Mavis and Estelle, along with him. He'd been in a big-time hard bop band but was old enough that he didn't care about pleasing anyone anymore. He just lived off the money he'd made off of shows in his earlier life and did cross-country gigs when he wanted to. That guy was fun and sloppy and fascinating, and Mavis loved how he just rumbled along, playing his tenor sax and putting down whisky, not giving a shit, always ending up with money somehow. Whether Mavis was bouncing around the Deep South with her uncle or finishing up undergrad at Xavier, she felt dull connections to cities. To most people too, outside of Estelle. After her uncle died, Mavis stayed in New

Orleans with Estelle so she could set up JazzFusion, a non-profit, with their college buds. Mavis wasn't a fan of working with other people, but JazzFusion helped promote the arts to kids, and that shit, she was for. That program lost its funding fast. Then Mavis and Estelle went to Miami, where Estelle tried the convent; then they went to Fort Pierce after Estelle ditched the convent. Estelle eventually scored a part-time job reading tarot for a has-been CMT darling in Nashville. Mavis moved to the city with her sister and reopened her nonprofit at a TSU-sponsored affiliate, but after two years, JazzFusion tanked a second time. Estelle wasn't doing too well either, her client dropped her, and she ended up taking a job at Coffee Crow downtown while searching for a new gig. When Mavis got offered a better gig as a research assistant at a museum in Kansas City, she took it. Estelle was staying behind. Mavis would likely fail in KC, alone, but at least she'd be someplace different.

Still, Mavis was here now, in Nashville. Sitting at a short table on the second floor of Bourbon Blues, looking over the iron-lace railing at the stage below. Here she was, feeling prickly in this New Orleans–themed boogie bar, at this going-away-party thing Estelle had planned for her. This thing Estelle and Skitt probably hoped would be tear filled or frothy with laughter. It wasn't. Mavis didn't want to hang out in some faux Louisiana club in Nashville. Mavis had already lived in New Orleans; she didn't need to be transported to a fake version of a place she knew intimately and had been also ready to leave. She didn't want to feel the weight of two failures and two cities she was sick of. She preferred to get wasted in the town house she and Estelle shared on Hillwood, far away from the girl on the stage, who Mavis loved.

The singer Mavis loved was called Beefie, and that girl was chatting with the band, laughing loudly, her smile boasting all of her brilliant teeth. Black Puerto Rican like Mavis's mami, Beefie was twenty-seven but acted like a sixteen-year-old. Scatterbrained as hell, always a little confused. Baby-faced with a birthmark on her cheek she hid with makeup. This girl was doing a mic check and nearly dropped the damn thing. Mavis had loved that girl longer than she wanted to admit, but her insides had done a good job of calcifying the emotion, making it something understandable, practical, manageable. Back when JazzFusion was still limping along and Mavis still had a job, she and Estelle went to scope out some bassist at Fanny's, to see if he wanted to teach a class. The sisters barged in on a practice session one day. Mavis was half-drunk; Beefie was in the front of the store, tuning a piano. She was belting out Otis Redding's "Tennessee Waltz" a capella, sang it so fine Estelle clutched her neck and Mavis got stung with viper-love. The day after, Mavis hooked Beefie up with a country guitarist on Broadway who needed someone to front his band. Within a month, Beefie was singing at Tootsie's and Blue-Girl nightly and pulling in fat tips. For the next two years, Mavis couldn't shake her feelings for that girl.

Tonight, Estelle waved at the singer, the bangles on her wrists clanging, near-hitting Mavis in the jaw. Beefie beamed big at the sisters. Her lavender eyes flashed, she pointed at Mavis and said, "I got you today, my favorite!"

Mavis rolled her eyes. Favorite. Sure. Beefie was too sweet, and it was infuriating. Only person in Nashville who'd ever made Mavis's belly flip. And here Beefie was grinning angel-like for Mavis. Mavis glanced at Skitt, the plaid-shirted hipster with a trailing Lord of the Rings beard, Beefie's new boyfriend. Skitt was sitting too close to Mavis; his lobby elbows kept sideswiping her when he clapped. He was watching Beefie too, his face all rainbows and light. Skitt jumped to his feet, clapping vigorously and almost hit Mavis again. She restrained herself from standing up and socking Treebeard in the fucking face.

Stop, woman, she told herself. Mavis massaged her temples. She still had too many reactions to shit like this. She'd never been a romantic. Mavis wasn't going to wind up with Beefie or make her happy. Mavis was a dick, and that wasn't going to change. Still, Beefie was an ever-present thorn, a scourge. That anguish settled into a dead nothing inside Mavis, so she just went along, readjusting the thorn when needed. Beefie stayed a friend, in the periphery.

Beefie was onstage, haloed by Fresnel lights and saying something to the drummer. She was too short for the periwinkle lace dress she'd thrown on.

Mavis snatched her sister's whiskey and downed half of it in one gulp. The shot burned Mavis's face and she felt perfect. When Beefie searched the crowd for Mavis's eyes. Mavis pretended to look for something in her pocket.

One shot wasn't enough. She turned around, checking for Hot Waitress. HW had been giving Mavis sweet looks and Mavis liked her. She had this blond-rose wig on and had been bumping into tables all night, which Mavis thought was kind of cute. But HW wasn't around, just some long-haired brunette waiter. He was medium height, which was short for six-foot-three Mavis. He saw Mavis looking his way and he wiggled his eyebrows. She raised her glass, and he nodded once, smiled with half of his mouth.

While Mavis was checking this guy out, the guitarist started blathering on. He was going on about how privileged they were to play on the Jimmy Hall stage, where B. B. King and James Brown once performed.

Estelle elbowed Mavis, tried to get her attention off the waiter and back to Beefie's show. Mavis ignored her sister and waved Cute Waiter over. CW sprinted to the table, pushed his chocolate eyes up in Mavis's face. He openly sized Mavis up, which she didn't like, but whatever. He saw her the way most straight guys did, a too-tall Black woman, cool and aloof. She fit the bill today in all black, with spikes in her eyes, a dark fedora, tight jeans, and knee-high boots. She was mowing through cigarettes and drinks, her face glowering a fuck-you to everyone. Most men didn't understand Mavis's energy, so they wanted to challenge her, see if they could soften her. They couldn't.

CW crossed his arms so Mavis could see the definition in his biceps. "What can I do for you, Grace Jones? Woman in Black? Miss Beyoncé?"

This was going to suck.

She threw an arm back over her chair, rattled the rings on her fingers. Maybe he'd be fun enough to waste time with, so she didn't have to focus on Beefie. Most of these Nashville guys were playing every girl on Broadway, so Mavis didn't feel bad about leading them on and dropping them before anything happened. Nashville dudes who weren't checking for Miranda Lambert knockoffs thought Mavis was hot and terrifying.

CW ran a hand through his hair. "I'll call you what you want. All I know is I love your vibe."

With the tequila hitting, Mavis felt pretty damn dashing. She was drunk enough that she could excuse the fact that this dude thought Beyoncé and Grace Jones looked the same, but he still had to earn her time, and he was failing.

"Yo," she said. "Do better. This ain't it. What else you got?"

He went on, unfazed. "Come on, I wanna know your story. How you ended up in this city. I noticed you immediately. You and that girl playing down there have to be the only . . ."

"Yeah?"

He blushed. "Ya'll are like unicorns in this town. You like unicorns?"

Mavis rolled her eyes. Forget it. She twirled her finger. "Look, kid. Whatever 'this' is? It's wack. Say something smart. Or get my order. It's tequila."

The guy shifted around in his boots. "Tough girl. Let's

chat later. You think you're hot shit, but I can go blow for blow."

"You can't even hold your own right now," she laughed. "Just get me my fucking drink."

He opened his mouth for a comeback that didn't come and she flapped her fingers. He tried again, but she threw him a bye-bye-buddy kind of look and he stamped away.

"Tequila, Papi. Remember it!" she called after him and whistled sharply.

Estelle wrenched Mavis's shoulder back to her. "What. Are you doing? *What was that?* Show some respect to your friends tonight. Please."

Mavis shrugged and lit a cigarette. Estelle clamped a hand over hers and pointed to the NO SMOKING sign. Mavis locked eyes with Estelle. She took a defiant draw, blew out a little puff of smoke over her sister's shoulder, and put the cig back in her pack. Estelle sighed.

Mavis didn't want to see Beefie's goodbye show. She wasn't going to enjoy it. Period. That girl was the worst combo, a Puerto Rican princesa living in the South who had double the traditional values. Her mami had been the side chick of some Puerto Rican mami's boy, and she had a complex about it with a capital *C*. Needed to be picked first but always wound up somebody's third. Beefie shouldn't even be interested in Mavis (and Mavis at least suspected she was interested) because Mavis picked herself first and second. Always. Beefie wanted a planned-out future, a bright wedding ring, and a barn. Mavis couldn't give her any of that and didn't plan to. Her feelings for Beefie had been hounding her long enough, and she was ready to leave the city and shake them out of her for good.

The guitar strings sizzled. D7/AG/G7. A spill of keyboard. Long whine of sax. Of course, Beefie was doing that damn Otis cover. They'd practiced it tons of times; Mavis and Beefie had shaped that thing together. Beefie had performed the Patti Page version at Tootsie's before; the band had mixed it spectacularly with Cash's "Tennessee Flat Top Box." Mavis had always liked Beefie's voice on Otis's cover best—it was Patti-high but scuffed with all of Otis's brusque longing.

Estelle squealed. CW tossed Mavis's drinks on the table.

Mavis put down the shot and it scorched her stomach quick. "Tip's on you," Mavis said to Estelle as the dude walked off.

"Thanks," Estelle said, rolling her eyes.

Onstage, Beefie cried, "This one's for my friend May! Here's to hoping she'll come back to Nashville soon!" Some of the crowd clapped politely. Some folks drunkenly coughed Mavis's name like they knew her. A few girls spun around to see who Mavis was, whispered something to their friends. The rest of the folks leaned into lovers, murmured orders to the shuffling waitstaff, gnawed on buffalo wings and alligator bites. Mavis looked at Beefie, even though she didn't want to.

Beefie, glowing under orange light, was killing that damn song. Of course she was. She was tearing Mavis's heart up awful; Mavis could feel her chest burning, aching, clenching with loss and the slow beauty of the song. Sorority bros were hollering, but the other folks stopped their talk; they wanted to see this girl croon about snatched-away love. Estelle put her hand over Mavis's knuckles, knowing everything. Mavis yanked her hand away. She didn't need pity. She was fine. Beefie was fine. The night was fine. Mavis wanted another shot. Where was that bro?

Beefie kept on singing. Rainbow lights streaked across the band. Skitt snapped photographs of his girlfriend with his pretentious-ass Rolleiflex and whooped. Mavis's insides toughened, got weak. Beefie was looking up into the balcony, and Mavis couldn't tell if she was looking at her or Skitt. Skitt, assuming it was him, mouthed, "Love you."

It was too fucking much. Mavis leapt up from her chair and Estelle got up too, said something like, *Don't*. Mavis held up a pack of Newports and ran down the spiral stairs. She pushed past the people on the floor, ran right past the stage where Beefie was still singing her away.

Outside, in the alley, under a drooping string of lights, Mavis lit another smoke. She watched drunk folks turtle in and out of Bourbon's open doors. Her wrists shuddered bad, and she caught her lighter from dropping twice.

Mavis felt lonely as fuck, even though she had folks waiting for her inside. Girls with white-blond hair curled to their asses wobbled along; taut-bodied Alabama bros pumped their fists. These folks were going to parade onto Broadway, whining and brawling, upchucking all over the Elvis statue in front of Country Life. How long had Mavis been snarling at these folks? Too long.

Mavis finished her cigarette, flicked it to the ground. She looked at the star-specked spread above Printer's. The sky laughed at her. It was blue, bitter, gloriously alive.

Mavis couldn't finish her second cigarette because, of course, there was trouble. Dumb trouble. She was trying to decide whether or not to go back inside or just walk around alone when Estelle sprinted out of Bourbon. Her patchwork skirt was swinging, silver bracelets banging. She ran up to Mavis, said, "Have you seen Beefie? Has she contacted you?" Estelle steadied herself on Mavis's arm and stumbled back, out of breath.

Mavis raised her eyebrows. Knowing Estelle, she was probably freaking out about nothing. She gestured with her cigarette to Bourbon's front door. "Nena, she's in the fucking club. Duh?"

Estelle threw her hands on her hips and shook her head, her big curls tumbling into her freckled face. "Listen to me! *Listen*. After you left, she couldn't finish. She just ran off the stage. She was crying. And now she's not anywhere."

Mavis pushed down a jolt of fear. "That girl can't drink for shit," she offered. "Probably put down too many daiquiris before the show and she's in a bathroom hurling her face out. Look harder."

"They checked all the bathrooms and backstage. You didn't see her run out?"

"No," Mavis shrugged, shook her head. "She could have slipped out the back."

"And her phone is off."

Mavis rolled her eyes. "Of course it is. Because she's a 'responsible adult.'"

"Beefie doesn't run out of shows," Estelle said, pulling her lips into her mouth and pushing them out. "That's not her. But now she's going to get this reputation . . ."

Mavis waved her hand. "Forget that. Let's just deal with the problem at hand."

Sure, Beefie lived for her music. Sure, Mavis had watched Beefie spend nights on their apartment floor memorizing Tootsie's set lists, writing her own songs, practicing her ad-libs. But that girl was ditzy as fuck. She lost her phone daily, had a staggeringly shitty alcohol tolerance and a penchant for sleepwalking. For all Mavis knew, Beefie had gone backstage to check on a sound glitch and tripped into a closet and was still in there. Estelle looked powerfully bothered, though, like she was worried about Beefie but also about Mavis. Her eyes kept roaming Mavis's face, up and down, sideways and longways, trying to figure Mavis out. Mavis looked away. She didn't like her sister's staring, and she didn't need advice.

"Anyway, we'll figure it out," Mavis said. Her head throbbed.

As if the night couldn't get more useless, Skitt showed up. The painterboy wandered into the group, nose to iPhone, his eyebrows knitted. He was swallowing over and over again, doing this annoying whistle thing with his mouth. "Hey, y'all," he said, without looking up. "Ugh, nothing. Beefie's not home."

Mavis reached in her pocket for her lighter. When Skitt said "home," it stung a little. The word conjured images of Skitt and Beefie clutching each other under body-warmed sheets. His wispy beard draped over Beefie's birthmark. She pushed the images out of her head. "This isn't serious," Mavis said to Skitt and lit the cigarette. "Stop," she waved the lighter. "You: whiteboy. Relax."

Skitt finally tore his eyes away from his phone. He said slowly, "My girlfriend is missing. I'm not going to 'relax.' Also, you're the supposed best friend who just ran out on your own farewell show. You have no idea how stressed she was about this, about impressing you and sending you off. Maybe you should *stop* 'relaxing.'"

Skitt got all pink in his hipster face. Mavis blew smoke into his eyes. He punched it away, threw his phone in his pocket. He started at her, like he wanted to do something, but didn't know what because Mavis was a woman, who towered over him, and she could definitely put that bitch in a headlock in T-minus one second. Estelle grabbed Mavis's shoulder and said, "Jesus, stop." Mavis ignored her and turned away. Skitt spit on the ground and spun around.

Fuck it. She left the group. She fell down on a bench by the club door close enough so she could hear them, far enough that she didn't have to deal with their bullshit, and finished her third cigarette. The two threw out what they knew. Skitt was Beefie's ride, so the girl couldn't have gone home. Beefie might have Ubered somewhere, but where? "Home?" She hadn't answered the landline. She could have gone to Broadway, where she worked and drank most weeknights, but there wasn't a clear reason why. Skitt didn't believe Beefie would have just left Bourbon Blues, so he decided to stay at the club. Estelle didn't know what to do, kept using words like "worried" and "anxious."

What a send-off.

Mavis's right eye was twitching fiercely and her chest felt bee-bitten, but she knew, in her gut, Beefie was fine. For all that girl's ditziness, she was capable. If other folks couldn't see that, Mavis could. That girl could hurl all over backstage before a set and go out and kill it. She had it. She didn't need Mavis.

After Skitt was securely inside Bourbon, Mavis got up.

"I'll check Broadway," she said to Estelle. "Was gonna go down there anyway. You wait with Skitt or go home."

Mavis didn't know if Beefie was on Broadway; she just wanted to be alone. She turned and started walking off, but Estelle floated to her side, hooked her arm around Mavis's. They went forward together.

Mavis and Estelle took a left on Fourth Avenue North, got off Printer's. They pushed past wasted folks and weekend strollers till the mouth of the street opened up to Broadway: electric and country, old and city-like. Broadway, with its lit-up boots, classic record shops, and neon guitar cutouts. With its trinket-full gift shops, faux saloons, and live karaoke bars featuring singers ready for radio. There it was: fat with screeching folks who smacked BBQ-wet lips and wondered, endlessly, where to get hammered. Mavis couldn't stand pageantry, and this place felt like a pageant. Or it felt like nowhere. Just another city to burn through.

Estelle zigzagged through people-full traffic. Mavis grabbed her wrist, got her to walk in a straight line.

"May. It's okay," Estelle said over a cover of some Dierks Bentley cut blasting from The Stage.

"Your navigational abilities? Not okay. Pretend you're on a tightrope, if that's easier."

"I'm saying . . ."

"I'm good," Mavis said, focusing on the road ahead of her. "You're a bumperkart, chica." Mavis gently guided Estelle by the shoulders away from a bouncer checking IDs.

"Whatever is surrounding you. The energy," Estelle said, breaking away from her. "It's muddy."

"Really?" Mavis turned around. "'Muddy'? Did the fucking Hierophant tell you that? Which God are you praying to now? All of 'em?" She dropped Estelle's wrist, and Estelle pulled roughly away. Mavis sighed a sorry. Her sister didn't deserve her shitty mood. They both went silent.

Tourists banged into the sisters, and Mavis shoved them away. Some bro slurred at Mavis, and she wanted to show him her fists but decided against it. She caught up with Estelle but didn't have much to say.

"Why aren't I like you?" Estelle said, finally.

Mavis furrowed her brow. "Man . . ."

"We had the same life. We're roamers. I can't have relationships either. Couldn't even keep a relationship with God. I dream of saying 'Fuck the world!' like you, but I can't. I feel so much, I can't feel anything. Too connected. To you, deeply, obviously. To everyone. Even Beefie. Even Skitt, who I just met. I feel like I'm drowning in emotions. Like now: I can feel how much you're hurting over Beefie. But you're so good at compartmentalizing. The love of your life has gone missing and you're like, 'Whatevs! Where's my fucking drink?' I wish I could do that. My brain's always trying to kill me." She shut her eyes tight, opened them.

Mavis stopped.

"First off," she said. "Nobody is the love of my life. Who knows how long your life will be, but nobody gets to claim the whole thing." They were walking side by side through the crowd again. "Second off, the love of your life is your fucking self, because she ain't going to leave you. You're stuck with her. Trust me, you don't want to be like me. Because the love of my life is a total bitch. And I love her. Punto y ya."

Mavis stuffed her hands in her pockets. She wasn't all that tough, and Estelle knew it, and she knew that Estelle knew it. Mavis was choked up with tangled emotions, just like her sister, especially right now. Those feelings got hard in her head and made her insane, but she wasn't going to let them out so everyone could stamp all over her and call her some weak Black woman. Give her tissues and shit. She'd gotten through life with a shield up like this, could protect Estelle like this. She liked herself. She wasn't changing.

Mavis tried to smile at her sister. She reached out and petted the smooth dark hair Estelle always let fall in her eyes. Mavis said, as tenderly as she could: "You're good, 'mana."

Estelle removed Mavis's hand from her head and squeezed it before she let her go. "I'm not saying you should change. I'm saying that sometimes some people should know how you feel. It's not always about you. And by some people I mean Beefie, when we find her."

"Okay."

"Okay?"

Estelle smiled. She was pointing to a bar where Beefie might be when Mavis's phone went off. Mavis scrambled to get it from her pocket. "Sofi Morales" blinked on the screen. Beefie's real name. Mavis'd given Beefie her nickname back when they'd first met. Mavis'd said something like, "Chica, you're so skinny, no meat on the bones. And for that: you get called Beefie." Beefie thought the name was funny, so it stuck.

Mavis's heart flew to her mouth. She cried out, too loud, "Hey? Hey?" Estelle got close to Mavis's phone.

They heard silence, glasses clinking, a chorus of drunk girls calling out each other's names.

The phone clicked off. Mavis called Beefie again, but she didn't pick up. Mavis cursed loud and stopped herself from chucking her phone at the sidewalk. Instead, she took off her hat and ran her fingers through her greased curls.

"You were right," Estelle said, placing a hot palm on Mavis's back. "She's on Broadway. Second floor."

Mavis put her hat back on, spat on the ground, turned to Estelle. "Your clairvoyance is working, huh?" Mavis suspected, after that call, Beefie was at Blue-Girl too. The only bar on Broadway Beefie would frequent on her own.

Estelle didn't smile. She studied Mavis's face, her forehead wrinkling. "Let's see if I'm right. Not about where she is. But why she left."

"You know that?"

"Of course I do. No clairvoyance needed."

Mavis pulled her lighter out of her pocket and lit another cigarette. She offered it to her sister. Estelle inhaled and exhaled the smoke peacefully.

In the Blue-Girl stairwell, Mavis and Estelle shoved their way around wide-mouthed, booze-happy folks. Bumper chords and twangy strings throbbed in the wooden walls. If Mavis hadn't been so irritated, she might miss the sounds of live country, the ubiquity of Nashville's cowboy culture. The sisters got off the stairwell and fell into yet another sweaty, packed crowd.

Mavis pulled Estelle through clamoring barfolks. She knew that wrist by heart, was happy for it. She tapped Estelle's hand and released her when they got to Blue-Girl's bar.

Mavis waved away the first two bartenders and called over Clive, a brown-skinned kid with pink hair. Mavis knew

Clive. He was a muscle-heavy stripper who worked the bar during Beefie's night gigs. They kept pledging to "get some BBQ or something" but never did.

"May!" he cooed. "I've missed you." His slippery pecs tensed as he wiggled his torso. "Can I . . ."

"Where's Beefie?" Mavis said.

Clive pointed to the stage.

Mavis turned and saw Beefie hunched over, clutching her knees on the three steps leading up to the stage, where the house band was finishing Hank's "Cold, Cold Heart." Beefie looked smaller than usual in a leather jacket; the lace of her hem was torn. She gazed dazedly at the singer above her, some country boy in green snakeskin boots.

When Mavis arrived at the stairs, Beefie didn't notice her. Mavis said, "Beefie," but didn't get a reaction. She called out the girl's real name, Sofia, rather Sofi Morales, and it tasted soft. Sofi. Hey, Sofi.

"Hey, Sofi," she said.

Sofi saw Mavis then. The girl's pale lips puckered.

"I'm sorry," Sofi said.

Mavis plucked her thumb at the door behind the crowd. "Let's talk?" she said. "Alley? Don't run off."

Sofi wiped her face, stood up.

Outside Blue-Girl, in another alleyway, Sofi leaned against the wall. She pulled out a Camel Blue, rolled it on her tongue. She was just flipping it and triple-eighting it in her mouth.

The whole performance pissed Mavis off. Was she playing with her? Mavis probably deserved it.

Mavis reached into her pocket, tossed the girl a lighter, and said roughly, "Vamo'."

Sofi caught the lighter but didn't use it. She looked at Mavis defiantly, kept that cigarette weaving up and down her tongue. Mavis got close enough to Sofi's face that she could feel the girl's cinnamon breath on her lips. The tongue-rolling stopped. Sofi's eyes shook, and Mavis reached over, yanked the cigarette out of the girl's mouth. Mavis lit it and started smoking, tasting Sofi's saliva all over the filter.

Sofi swallowed, audibly.

"Why'd you go?" Mavis said. Sofi shoved her hands in her pockets and stared at a halved bottle on the ground.

"I couldn't finish the song."

"The band's gonna be pissed at you," Mavis said, exhaling smoke. "Gave the only Blatina in the city, jazz singer at that, a chance in this country band. And you fuck it up. You know what they say about you. Now that failure is on you. Me too, but you know I don't give—"

"I know," Sofi said, her eyes darkening. "You don't give a shit." She squirmed against the brick. She reached into her pocket, pulled out her dead phone, drew circles on it with her forefinger.

Mavis didn't know what else to say.

Mavis could still hear the Blue-Girl singer. She'd moved on to another Cash song, an old one, back when the Man in

Black was courting June. The folks on the street were laugh-crying, and everybody, somewhere, was singing something.

"I spent all week practicing," Sofi said to her shoes.

Mavis took another drag from Sofi's Camel. "Sorry. I'm an asshole."

"No. I just wasn't good enough. You can always tell when I'm not doing my best, when I'm making mistakes. That's why you left."

"Nah." She softened and said, "You were actually—beautiful." Mavis avoided eye contact, pretended to flap away the smoke in front of her.

Mavis immediately regretted how she'd used that word. Fuck *beautiful*. Mavis wasn't the kind of person who used *beautiful* unless she was being sarcastic. She wanted to shove the *beautiful* back in her mouth.

Still, Mavis saw it, the red flash in Sofi's eyes, the chin twitch. The story Mavis probably knew without anyone telling her. Sofi ran out because she was hurt Mavis took an impromptu smoke break during her show. Because Sofi loved Mavis too.

"There's too much changing," Sofi said.

"Nothing is changing for you," Mavis said. "You've got this. World at your feet, tigresa. Platitudes, platitudes."

Sofi let out a breath. "Everything stayed firmly in place because you were around."

Mavis laughed sharply. "No. I'm not part of anything. I'm just watching y'all live brightly from the shadows."

Sofi pinched her temples. "That's not true at all. You really matter to me. To Estelle too. We really need you. Want you. You know."

Mavis swallowed, stepped away from Sofi. She wanted to yank the girl to her thin chest. Or run out of the alleyway, never to see Sofi again.

"Hey," Mavis said. "I'm leaving. And that sucks. Because I probably love you. But that's life, you know. Qué será, se—"

Sofi's dead phone smacked the ground. Her eyes were huge and orange, and she didn't say anything. That unreadable look made Mavis feel naked, ugly. Mavis straightened her face; she tried to look tough.

"Are you kidding me?" Sofi said.

"Yo, chica, you hungry?" Mavis said. "Let's get some wings at Brother Z's. Uber's on me." She shouldn't have said a thing; her whole body felt like a wound torn open.

"You had two years!" Sofi said, her voice rising nearly hysterically. "I couldn't sleep. I got ill with feelings. But you were always around someone else, and you didn't see me, but then you'd be looking at me, and it felt so terrible because I could tell you were looking."

"Nah. You were fine."

"Then I met Skitt. My singing got better. I got brighter. You saw that. But the whole time, you were just . . ." Her face burned, her eyes filling. "Not changing." She glared at Mavis with a mix of contempt and yearning. "Just being yourself . . ."

Everything Sofi was saying was perfect and wretched.

Sofi'd said everything Mavis wanted to hear, even the cold parts. Of course, Mavis wanted to stay. And that would be stupid. Mavis would rather be a lesson learned for this girl, not the reason Sofi's life got upended.

So Mavis shrugged one shoulder. "I didn't know, man. Missed connections, all that. It happens."

Sofi let out a breath. She turned to the wall, yelled at it, then turned around. She spun back around and kicked a pebble. The rock hit Mavis's shin, lightly. Yeah, Mavis could just rush over, bury her nose in that girl's velvet neck. But she wouldn't. This was all pointless.

"I'm healthy," Sofi said, breaking her eyes from Mavis. She looked like she was weighing something. "And you're leaving. And who knows if you're coming back."

"I'm not. Not for you," Mavis said. She could have added something romantic, but she didn't.

Mavis looked out at Broadway's hot streets. A family in Predators jerseys and plastic pink boots strode by. A few coils of Estelle's black-brown hair stuck out of the alley mouth. Her sister was waiting for her, as she always was. Mavis pulled out her wallet, counted two hundred dollars, and took her phone out. She pushed the money and cell into Sofi's hands, broke away before she could feel the girl's skin.

"Call Skitt. Let him know you're alive." Mavis tore the Camel out of her mouth, tossed it to the ground. She stamped the thing out. She wanted to cry right there; she hadn't cried in a long time. How long? Since that sax man died. Estelle was the weeper, not her.

Sofi made a tiny sighing sound, and Mavis refused to look up and see her lips. "Apologize to your band," Mavis said to the alley floor. "Give them that two hundred bucks. Promise two more shows, for half. I'll pay the difference. I'm gonna snag Estelle, get plastered at our place. You're welcome to drink with us." Mavis walked off, not knowing if Sofi was behind her or not.

Hours later, at Mavis's townhome on Hillwood, Skitt, Estelle, and Sofi drank hard. Skitt invited some hipsters over from East Nashville. Estelle brought out a twenty-buck karaoke machine so Sofi could sing some eighties pop. Mavis fixed a pot of chunky gumbo for everyone but didn't drink. She watched the girl she loved get plastered. Watched Sofi purposefully butcher Cyndi Lauper. She watched Estelle wow the shawled and bearded boys with her tarot; Mavis watched all those folks finish off her stew.

The group fell asleep, happy and warm-bellied. Mavis thought about rousing Sofi, but she was snoring in Skitt's arms. Mavis dozed off on the leather couch and woke up early when the sky turned pink. She took two packed bags to her '98 Sentra and climbed inside. What a fine feeling: the thud of ass to car seat, the swift rush of freedom that came from sitting in a small space alone. Mavis started the engine.

Estelle opened the house's front door. She stood on the yellow porch in bunny slippers and a cotton robe. Her sister-friend: looking like some kind of home. Behind her stood

Sofi. The girl's eyes were red, the makeup from the night wiped off. Mavis could see the birthmark, beautiful, on her left cheek.

Mavis decided to cry when she got back to the hotel. She'd cry long and wild for hours until everything was out, finally. And then she'd move on. For now, Mavis raised a hand and loved those women. She pulled out of the driveway, got back on the road.

Last Saints

Present (Baton Rouge, 1932)

THE MOMENT SHAFFER "POTATO" GREGGS HOBBLED into Sweet Heaven Saloon, he wanted to turn on his heels and scoot. Greggs's spirits, already pit-low, deepened into a dejection so fantastic, he wished he could trap it in a mason jar.

Greggs hated Sweet Heaven. The place was too hot, trash-stuffed, and funky as feet. Satan's crotch, he thought. Damn place is like rubbing my face in Satan's crotch. He yearned for his homeplace's juke joints. In Emmaus bars, men and lady-folk joined to laugh hard and lindy hop, to pack their mouths with hearsay and cut-up franks. The folks in Emmaus weren't good, exactly, but they didn't plot out meanness or deceit. If a man staggered home with a shoeless shopgirl in hand, he didn't intend to use her. He just wanted some sable skin to hide his face in, a smile to tell his secrets to. She just wanted a safe night with a country man who'd tell her good lies. An Emmaus gathering went something like this: Old men, wrinkled gals, fresh-skinned ladies and boys, all those folks' mouths flapping open with happy love breaths. Those folks wriggled, twisted, flicked their black knees, skated to the right and left, killed bayou floors with roughed-up shoes. Emmaus joints had true sweetness and maybe a bit of heaven. Still, this not-home, this Sweet Heaven Saloon existed, and a storm washed Emmaus away. So that was something.

At a quarter after eleven, the bells above the door clanged loud. As Greggs tottered inside, the customers smirked with chicken skin fixed between their front teeth. Eh, ho! they sang, Country goat, country goat! Yah don't belong, go get gone! They were right. Greggs didn't belong on these greasy, shoe-stained tiles. Not underneath the lights, subsuming the dance floor in a smoky devil-red he could taste. Not around men as old as he smacking their thighs for a young singer crooning bluesy epics. He didn't belong with these boys either, with their shimmering blond suits, slimy curls pressed beneath colossal flopping hats, toothpicks protruding from flimsy teeth. They laughed with pretzels in their mouths and spit, crunched, spit. He didn't know these ladyfolk, with their sticky, fried hair, their skin slathered with ocher cream, their double-drop earrings swinging, sparkling. Greggs was not like them at all. A country fellow he was, over eighty and underdressed, with gray skin, bulbous cheeks, and a half-steady gait. He navigated the floor with a walking stick, his legs performing shivery waltzes. His shirt was buttoned to his neck, his head mammoth. He wore lace-less rubber shoes and worn hemp-cloth pants, known to city folk as "slave slacks." He told them straight, he wasn't a slave.

You know where you at? Stray voices cackled, Hey ho, country goat!

Greggs ignored them. He focused on the girl he had come for, the one Ol' Brujie told him was still in the state. The one he couldn't believe was at this not-home place now, pinching the stem of a crystal glass, wetting her teeth with plum wine. After ten years, he hoped that girl would be somewhere up North, cleaning up some proper folks' home. Maybe learning Something Important, her mouth pursed as she scribbled notes for a Dr. Somebody's lecture.

She shouldn't be here.

He noticed her back first, a long stretch of tight skin, the shade of a tupelo dipped in night. Her legs were crossed, a red heel halfway off her foot, her hamstring muscle tense and protruding.

Country goat done lookin'! Nah, goin' nah, country man!

Greggs swallowed and tried a few steps forward.

This girl was not that little girl. That little girl, the girl he was ordered to protect, was thirteen, not twenty. His girl could not be this smooth, sugar-scented feline with hellfire eyes. His girl's back needed to be miniature and curved. She should have skinny thighs and doorknob knees. Her hair should be coiffed and curled underneath her chin. This girl, not little, wore a backless dress that led a man's eye from neck to naked spine. This girl was not sweet Red from Emmaus.

Greggs rubbed his lips and walked over to the young woman's seat. He wanted to look spiteful, intimidating, but his face was damp and he couldn't control his fingers.

The girl lowered her glass, sensing a body. She turned gradually, coquettishly to meet him, expecting some admirer who would offer her hot talk and a long drink. When the girl recognized Greggs, her bottom lip dropped, revealing a wet gum.

Greggs tried to swallow but his throat was too dry. The woman's eyes flashed, narrowed, settled into a glare.

"Damn it, Potato," she spit.

Her face still retained the roundness of youth, the chin mostly, and her little lips, now painted a blinding scarlet, still had the plumpness he remembered.

She called him Potato. Yes, that was his Emmaus name. His best name, probably. Potato blinked, tried a few weak words, but he failed to say anything good. He tried once more, croaking:

"Hey. Chile. Been trying to find you."

The girl snarled, threw her arms across her breast, and leaned forward. "Man, I ain't no chile. Did I ask you to come find me? No. Walk your skinny ass 'way from me. Now."

The muscles of Potato's jaw fluttered. Of course he shouldn't have come. He should have stayed in Calcasieu. At least there, he had that one-room cabin he'd built from cypress scraps all by himself; at least there the sharp scent of deadwood comforted him. To find this girl, he had to interact with other folks, and he didn't like other folks. To find her, he had to lose a month of his savings from field work and two weeks' pay. Regardless, even if he weren't justified, even if he were mad, even if he didn't know why he came, he felt justified because he spent so much on the ferry and wasted all this time embarrassing himself in Sweet Heaven.

"You don't got no right to tell me where I can go," he said. "I got the right to be here and anywhere, long as there ain't no sign that says 'No Colored Folks' or 'No Potato.' So I'ma sit down, and you can do whatever you do." Potato lowered himself on to the stool beside the young woman. He steadied himself with his cane until he was securely in his seat.

The girl watched him, visibly disgusted. "Christ. Jesus Christ. You look bad, Potato. Spent all them years bein' foul to your body and now you look foul. Look like you about to fall into a grave."

So she was a mean girl now too. Didn't matter. Young folks thought they could say any damn thing when their heads were full of nothing. Potato shrugged and beckoned the bartender. He ordered a whiskey and asked the shiny-faced man if the place had sweetbread. The bartender shook his head, the corners of his mouth flicking up. He turned around to find a glass, chuckling.

"Sweet Heaven don't got no type of your bread, fool," the girl said. "This ain't Emmaus."

Potato snatched his drink from the bartender and tried a fast gulp. The liquor burned down his throat. "I can't remember you ever being this nasty, Sugar Red." He wiped his lips and laid his elbows on the table. "Can I call you that, or you got some new name now? Something explaining why you here and the unholy way you acting toward an old man?"

"Fuck you," she said. Potato didn't react. Although her black cheeks were blazing red, the girl hadn't stamped away from him yet.

Potato smiled small. "Found a foul mouth," he said. "What's wrong with you? Can't imagine Booey'd ever approve of . . ."

Booey. The color drained from the girl's skin and Potato put down too much of his whiskey, too quick. He shouldn't have said that name, should have bitten the word dead.

Her piping voice was tiny now. "I ain't like y'all. My name ain't Sugar Red. I'm Thea. That's my real name. Mama-given, not given to me by no town or no Booey."

"All right."

"And I ain't as terrible as you think, Potato. You should believe me," she said. The ghost of Little Sugar Red overtook Thea, just for that moment. Potato didn't know if he wanted to see that girl again. He thought, then: Why the hell am I here?

"I got money now." Thea's voice stiffened as she regained her composure. "Much more than you, I bet. You judgin' me, judgin' me in my dress, judgin' me in my new ways, and I know you be thinkin' things like you my daddy. Watch it now, 'cause you wrong. See, I ain't one of them gals that let some filthy nigger feel me all over. No, I ain't no coon, and I don't get trapped in no coon trap. I'm a skillful lady. And bein' a colored woman you need skills, bein' so vulnerable in a world with so many leeches. Right? Right. I seen many a great thing, Potato, met so many interesting folk I woulda never met if I had stayed till the end of Emmaus. Man, I was with one man, a boxer . . . watched him win ten matches in a row, come up with just a bloody nose. Kid shorter than February showed me how to get dollars from dogs rippin' up other dogs' necks. Even met skinny twins who could bend and twist like funny putty. And another fellow—he were a northern Negro who only wore blue suits—he taught me to read and gave me words like 'vit-too-perative' and 'spee-she-ush.' I stole some more words from him, but I can't tell you 'em. I believe you'd snatch them away."

"That's fine, Sugar Red."

Thea ignored his refusal to use her real name. "You said you might go back to Emmaus then. Did you?"

"Naw," Potato said. "Nothing there but drained-out swamp, knocked-over cypress. Why go?"

"You could have done something. Helped rebuild. You was such an Emmaus-lovin' man."

Potato rubbed his mouth. "Well, I didn't. Why you playing with me?"

Thea picked a little pimple underneath her left ear. "When I heard about the storm, I thought: good. Thought God was telling Emmaus, 'Y'all niggas need to be taken out!' Like Emmaus was Sodom. Like that place Noah was from."

Potato pinched his brow, his head flaming from the whiskey. "Foul."

"Shoo. Foul. Maybe you shoulda left my foul ass there,

then. Maybe you think I'm the kind of evil that needs to be wiped out."

Potato leaned forward, kept the edge on his voice soft. "You watch it, gal."

"Watch it? Watch it," Thea laughed. "You know what? If you was gonna save my life, you shoulda given me all you had. That's what you shoulda done. You can't just give a lonely little girl half of everything. You shoulda given me all of your money, all your time. All of it. I was sad, very sad having to leave my home. Having to leave my poor grandmamma. I was always crying. You shoulda given me everything."

Potato sucked his teeth. He'd set her up with his cousins in Leonville after the Booey mess. His kin were soft-souled folks. It wasn't his fault that girl ran off and ended up in a place like Sweet Heaven. She was ignoring what really happened.

"I bet you was real sad."

Thea was in the process of countering Potato, but she stopped. The girl's fingers fluttered on the table; her irises jigged about their eye-skins. "Potato . . . ," she started, leaning toward him, her mannerisms softer. "What you mean?"

"By what?"

Thea blinked four times and hid her hands underneath the table. "By . . . what you just said. You talking like you think something."

"Think what?"

"Like you think I did That Bad Thing to Booey."

Potato said nothing. He felt old now, older than Moses and Abraham and the prophets themselves. Potato frowned and watched nasty men weigh the weight of Thea's breasts. If he had more energy he'd knock them folks out, but he didn't. They just moved on to the next girl. Potato saw, knew too goddamn much. She didn't know a thing, that girl, who was once just a little child from his beloved home.

Potato thought, then: Why the hell am I here?

Potato and Thea both thought: We rememberin' That Night, ain't we?

That Night:
Potato's First Memory (Emmaus, Louisiana, 1926)

Ol' Booey always said to Potato, "Your home, like your name, it's in you. Whether you like it or not. Wherever you go, your name, your home gonna stay stuck in you."

On That Night, Potato'd been thinking about the nickname Emmaus gave him. About hating it. Every evening, Potato, always chewing on his thoughts, tramped the town's cypress woods, chewing, chewing, as the moon chipped into the tree branches, and his brow got wet from the huge hot air.

Potato. Poh-tate-oh. Many of the townsfolk boasted a name absent from their birth certificate, usually reflective of the person's most recognizable attribute, but Potato deserved better. At least he thought so. Nobody was sarcastic when they called the smooth-skinned Selene "Pretty Sally"; everyone knew Sweetie (or Marcus G) was sweet on all of the gals; and Paris Toads of Toads Grocery had never been to Paris, but he quoted French limericks like a college man. There was Booey too, but nobody knew her birth name. Booey was Booey. Nobody asked questions about her past. Booey was sacred, a prophetess and matriarch to all of Emmaus. In any case, those names were not terribly derisive. At least Potato felt that way.

Nobody cared that Potato was actually Shaffer Greggs. He had been Potato since birth.

Potato, Potato, looks like a potato, here come potato-headed boy!

Potato preferred "Woodsman" or "Hunter." Even "Tree-Cutter." He always assumed the townsfolk were un-appreciative of his place in Emmaus, ignoring his any-time-of-the-doggone-day commitment to clearing brush, hacking tangled moss from windows, and dragging halves of oak to empty places for home building. Potato, Potato, cut my trees, Potato! The only two folks who noticed his efforts were the magical old Booey and her granddaughter Thea, or "Sugar Red." Before Booey's heart hollowed out from sadness, she embodied the heart of Emmaus. The townsfolk thought Booey's counsel was prophet-like, that she was the mouth of Somebody's God. She was the one who said, "God don't frown on you, Potato." She was the one who told Potato, "You a golden man!" when he rebuilt Booey's Special House.

Special House was both Booey and Emmaus's treasure, a lilac-colored, hipped-roofed Acadian at the far edge of the town, where swamp gave way to spring. When Potato had assessed the damage after the first storm—the bruised roof, the glass on the floor, and the dismantled doorframes—he grinned and bragged, "I can refix this place without a doubt,

Booey." And Booey embraced him, absorbing him into her clouds of chestnut dough. She whispered in his ear, "You a saving man, Shaffer Potato."

Booey lost her faith when she lost those two boys to Ray's dogs. Her earth-hued eyes muddied; she pursed her lips shut. She no longer spoke glorious words, no longer said much at all. Booey was neither cruel nor cold; she simply was. Potato blamed Ray Blake; Booey's end began with that fool.

Nobody liked Ray Blake. Ray was Booey's adopted son from her dead ladyfriend, and he didn't resemble his surrogate mother in any way. He was steel-eyed, salt-tongued, and infamous for dirty business. Ray couldn't keep a coin in his pocket; he often stole from Booey and eventually ran away at nineteen, only to return three years later to ask for more cash. He disappeared for another ten years, before finally stumbling onto Booey's porch on an Easter eve with a stringy wig, asking for money to buy a shack by the river. After receiving the loan, Ray stayed away from Booey for a long time, until he overheard gossip that she was writing a will, and Special House would be bequeathed to Booey's grandchildren (but not the girl Thea nor her mother for some reason), along with the land. Ray had always dreamed of owning the house. In a rage, he rushed over to Booey's place. Fortunately, Booey had changed the locks, in anticipation of Ray's anger. Ray, though, wouldn't accept defeat. Every other evening, the coal-colored, sphere-bellied man would round Special House, roaring, Hey, Boooey, heyyy, Booooey, how you play me? Why you play me? Potato, along with many other

townsmembers, tried to chase the man away, but Ray got two
pit bulls from a neighboring town and held the animals on a
leash whenever he circled Special House. After that, nobody
dared touch Ray; those dogs were demon beasts, screeching
and slathering all over the yard.

Potato had been trying to devise a plan to shoot the things
down, when he got the news the dogs had somehow loosed
themselves from Ray's fence and somehow found their way to
gobble up the heads and necks of Sugar Red's brothers. Since
the Law ignored Emmaus and the town's one sheriff was near
half-dead, Ray wasn't arrested. A group of townsmen simply
raided Ray's shack and shot his dogs to death in his own yard.
Still, Emmaus blamed Ray, and each week they attempted
to force him out of town. Ray refused to leave and admit
it was his fault. "Them dogs had a mind of they own," he
would snarl and then add, "them children shouldn't been out
at night looking for trouble. Trouble's a hungry thing, and it
ain't my fault Trouble got its belly rumblin'."

In any case, Ray stopped harassing Booey for a while because now she was broken, and even he could not handle Booey
in ruins. Booey had loved those babies with a soul-heavy love,
the kind of love that's so outrageous it's nasty, and everybody
knew it. Not even Missy, Red's and the twins' mother, was de-
stroyed like Booey. Missy had no choice but to gather her bear-
ings and live on for her daughter—at least that's what Potato
thought. Potato prayed Booey would recover from her heartbreak over those boys, but she didn't. Her heart supported all

the hopes of Emmaus, and Potato guessed she was too old and soul-tired to fuel that machine in her chest anymore.

Sugar Red was the only grandchild of Booey who lived. Potato thought her nickname was lovely and appropriate, since her brown cheeks blushed easily and she had a kindly temperament. She was the girl who chuckled when the woodsman grumbled about being named Potato and giggled, "Well, I wouldn't mind being called Potato. Fact, I love potatoes. I'd be Red Potato . . . fine with butter and cream." He laughed along, feeling light and silly and magical. Those two were so precious to a lonely woodsman without a mother or father or wife.

Which is why, on That Night when Potato came to Booey's house and saw that terrible scene, the thoughts he'd been chewing blew from his brain and into the green air. He stopped thinking about his nickname.

Before That Night:
Sugar Red's First Memory (1922–1924)

Booey always told Sugar Red: "Your mama didn't get it much, but the place you live is the place gonna stick in you, it gonna show like a busted lip. You gonna be an Emmaus memory everywhere you go."

Before That Night, before Sugar Red fled Booey in the bushes, she didn't think much about her Emmaus-ness.

Emmaus was just her home. Not wonderful, not magical, but fine enough.

Red knew Southern Louisiana's wet heat, so moist her hair roots shrunk up the moment she skipped outside of Mama's door. She'd trot by quarter-cabins with walls too thin to entrap the voices rattling the pots in Some Lady's kitchen. Her cloth shoes would go pat pat on red clay roads as she sprinted past women holding bags fat with lard cans and leeks, women who would return home and cook up an ugly supper that tasted so fine. She'd laugh at Ol' Baby Licker and Sweetie quarrelling in front of Sweetie's Grocery. Baby would yell, "Your meat price so high, Rockefeller hisself wouldn't touch your ham with his golden stick!" and Sweetie would return, "You don't know Rockafellah! Take me to his home, man!" And there was Ms. Pillow, her mama's best pal, a woman as large and lighthearted as her name. "Ooh Lord, the news!" She'd wheeze, "Lord, the news!" Ms. Pillow had the best Cajun diner in town and was the first to spread the news when Ray's dogs died.

Potato, too. She knew him well. He'd take Sugar Red and her brothers up the hill to Special House. "Cute li'l Red, if you ever need a thing you call me and I'll appear like poof . . ." Potato would pledge things like that. He'd lean down and pat Red's head and say, "Know I'd do anything for Booey's baby." Red would grin and kiss his cheek politely. She pitied him. Potato was the sort of fellow folks forgot quickly unless they needed him, and he seemed terribly dependent on folks needing him. As Thea got older, she grew irritated with Potato's meekness and senseless devotion to Booey (who always overinflated his ego), but she didn't see the point in ignoring him. He was just so damn sad.

Pathetic Potato. So attached to Booey, so unaware of the old woman's mind. Red knew Booey's true thoughts. She remembered Booey murmuring to her in private, "All of them in this town are my wayward lambs. They'd never survive without me." That Booey was always playing savior, always thinking she was some Black Lady-Jesus. Booey was double-faced, Thea believed, even before Ray's dogs tore apart her brothers' heads. This is the reason why:

When Red first got to know Booey (without a multitude of dreary, miracle-hungry townsmembers), she was eight. Mama said to Thea, Percy, and Bo, "Your grandmamma called for all of you, says she saw something with her Seeing Eye." Mama was a disturbingly quiet woman with a body as skinny as her sentences. Her skin was earth-colored, her eyes pallid. She wasn't Booey's original daughter. Like Ray, Mama belonged to Booey's collection of forgotten babies. Red's mother was a gentle, childlike woman, who was maybe fiercely stupid, as Red never remembered her mother disagreeing with anything or anybody. On that day, Booey spoke with her grandchildren in Prophesy Place, a circular clearing Potato had made by hacking down live oak and using the leftover stumps for friends—or, more appropriately, "worshippers"—to sit upon. After Booey removed her shoes and lowered herself onto the largest, most polished stump, she instructed Mama to go back to Special House. Red's mother nodded meekly, and the girl and her brothers folded their legs near their grandmother's feet, their tiny ankles wriggling with anticipation. Palmetto bugs bleated from shagbark; long-haired oil beetles shook off sweat. The sun sat down with Booey on her big stump. Percy poked Bo, Bo poked Red, Red poked both; they all pressed their hands together.

Booey spread her arms, slabs of heavy skin flapping back and forth. She proclaimed: "These are some holy words I only tell my grandbabies. My specials, now you goin' know my visions and truths."

Red's young heart quivered at the word *truths*, a majestic word even more marvelous out of Booey's mouth.

She talked to Percy and Bo first. "Pretty chile angels . . ." Booey gathered the boys into her arms then kissed their collarbones. She sighed, smashing the children into her huge breast. She smelled their ears and cheeks and scalps. After a few moments, the boys could no longer breathe and the woman released them, her face hot with light. Booey said:

"All good is in you, my babies, all good."

Red's small fingers trembled; her pulse pushed through her wrists. What about her? What would Booey say of her?

Booey furrowed her mole-specked brow, silver slivers flipping in her eyes. She advanced toward her granddaughter and stretched her fingers. "Thea. Sugar Red." She grasped Red's shoulders. Booey's nails cut through Thea's frock with a savage grip. Booey had never been so rough with Percy and Bo.

"Can't love you like them, baby girl," she said. "I gots to love those boys most. 'Cause of their spirits. I foresee 'em doing wondrous things someday. Problem with you, little Red, is Satan put up a nice home in your soul. And he living in that house hard, just like he lived in your mama when I found her four years older than you, stomach full of a baby she got from some clerksman who got to runnin'. I took that child to the river. Know why? This is why: I had to teach your mama how to make her kin the right way. With a husband. But still your mama didn't have no spirit that could change. You were blessed you all had a daddy. And he still died of her sin. Your daddy's illness was her illness, I bet."

Red wanted to say something, but her insides were throbbing with hurt.

Booey went on, "Baby girl, all women bear the sin of Eve, the sin of loving things that can only be held in a hand. Some women struggle and win against they evil, but I don't believe you one of them few. And since you are like my blood kin, I say careful. Careful, careful."

After that day, Red was not careful. She pushed her rejection, Booey's stupid prophesy, down low and deep. Booey never told the town of what she really thought of Red, and Red didn't have to tell. Booey's kin had to be publicly holy; the old woman wanted it that way. So all of Emmaus called Thea "Sugar Red" and thought she was wonderful because Booey (supposedly) loved her. From then on, Sugar Red directed all of her hurt on Booey and her own brothers, who had slowly separated themselves from their sister, frightened by her (supposedly) dormant evil. Booey was a hypocrite. She'd always call the women "sisters," and "blessed," never "all females got evil." But still, how Thea yearned for Booey's praise! How she yearned for that Ol' Fat Liar to love and bless her.

After Ray's dogs ravaged Percy and Bo, Thea no longer visited Booey with her mother. Mama didn't have the energy to travel up the heat-doused woods to visit an elderly woman without a soul. The town mourned the loss of Booey's smile more than the grandbabies themselves. Not Percy, not Bo. Just Booey, Booey, Booey. Nobody cared about Thea. Those boys were her brothers, but nobody cared that her knees slammed and knocked when some folk named Alfonso Marquez burst in Mama's house and announced the news. She loved her brothers despite the fact that she was deemed too filthy to be like them. Nobody cared how Thea mourned. Or even how Mama mourned, how her body lost the last bit of its tiny weight and the wind lifted her bones into the slate-colored sky. This new Booey who arrived after her brothers' death was worse than the first; the new woman only spoke to invoke fear. Like this: Her lips flopping and hopping and shuddering with nothing-stuff. Like this, she said: "The dogs, they comin' to get me, they comin', comin'!" And the town wailed, "Booey will rise again! Let's wait! Let's cry for her! Oh, oh, she will . . . if not, what will become of us?"

They were fools, Thea thought. Or desperate to keep this town of former slaves and darkfolks alive. They didn't realize Booey was just some folk, like anybody else; she didn't embody a damn thing.

That Night:
Potato's Second Memory (1926)

On That Day, Sugar Red's mother, Missy, said:

"Potato, when you walk out tonight, will you see if you catch my baby? I let her take some cakes she made to Booey, but I done wish I hadn't now. I don't want her back so late." And Potato replied:

"Yes, ma'am, my pleasure. She'll be safe; I'll keep a good eye on her."

Potato wished he'd kept both eyes on Red, not just the good one. The bad one and the good one together might have helped him find a faster pathway to Booey's house. One good eye did just as much as one good leg. Not enough.

On That Night, Potato's promise felt impossible. His body was fixed in Booey's doorway, his feet fastened to the floor-boards. Potato could not see the furniture or the house decor, but his nostrils burned from feet smells and the piquancy of blood he recognized from years as a huntsman.

Potato clutched the doorpost. "Thea, baby? Booey, girl?" He tried again hoarsely, releasing his fingers, one by one, from the door. "Miss Booey! Thea, baby?"

He pitched his lanky body into the blackness and felt through the dark.

He bumped and tripped and fell and returned to his feet, then bumped and tripped again. All the while Potato called their names, both of them. BooeyRedBooeyRed.

In what looked like a hallway, a heart-shaped window

clanged open, moonlight flaking onto the head of a girl with apple-bright cheeks. She was on the floor, smashed into a corner in some shrouded area of Special House. The girl was hunched over, her small arms enwrapping miniature legs.

My gal's alive. Joy should have softened Potato's fear, but his fear was too sticky. He could not see "his" girl's eyes or face. She was underneath those doll-sized arms. He could not see her face and understand the horrible thing that had occurred, and he knew it was horrible because he was no longer chewing thoughts.

"Hey there, Sugar Red . . ."

With a tinkling noise in her mouth, Red said, "Oh, Potato."

"Damn. It's so black in here, girl . . . where Booey at?"

At the mention of Booey, the girl wrenched her head upward to match Potato's gaze. The woodsman stepped back, suppressing a gag.

Sugar Red was no longer Sugar Red. Although her signature features were still the same, this child was no longer a child. Her hair, once fixed in two soft braids, now burst from her scalp in wild knots. The eyes, the worst, reflected a wretched green-brown, like the puke tucked beneath the stools in Toads' Bar.

"Booey ain't here," she said. "His hounds got her."

"Baby . . ." Potato swallowed, backing farther away from Sugar Red. "Them dogs is long dead."

The girl shook her head and snapped her eyes shut. When she opened them again, the vomit color in her eyes was

replaced by a film of tears. "You wrong. They got my brothers, now they got her. They tried to get me too. Look at me,
huh? His dogs was all inside me. And Booey got eaten, and I
got eaten a little too, but now you here and they gone somewhere aways . . ."

Bit by bit Potato lowered his knees to the floor. He reached
for Sugar Red, but his fingers stalled in the air.

"Not his dogs . . . you mean Ray hurt you?"

"No, sir. His dogs."

Potato's nose felt too stuffed. He couldn't breathe with
all that snot. He needed a tissue, a handkerchief. "I got to
sneeze," Potato said absently, and then, "Ray done got Booey.
Tell me plain, Sugar. Don't protect him."

"His dogs got her, yessir."

"Listen, gal . . . them dogs is dead. We killed 'em 'while
back. You sayin' Ray bought new dogs?"

"No, sir. They the same. Didn't see no Ray."

Potato lifted his elbow and sneezed into his arm. He
wiped the mucus away with his fingers carefully, thoroughly,
as if the task required his utmost attention.

"Red. This is real important. You telling me the truth?
The God-Jesus-Paul-Moses-Mary-Martha truth?"

"Potato, sir, I wouldn't tell no lies."

"No, you wouldn't."

"I wouldn't. You know me, Potato, sir."

And Potato did know her, didn't he? Even though she,
too, had three names.

That Night:
Sugar Red's Second Memory (Emmaus, Louisiana, 1926)

On That Night, as Sugar Red clumped down the dirt path to Special House, her brow soaked and shiny, Ray's voice bellowed from the cypress woods:

"Hey, girl! Smells like something love-made in that basket!"

That Day, the cala cakes Sugar Red made for Booey were not glazed with love. Rather, the cakes, honey-dribbled and coughing up with sweetness from the handkerchief by her side, had been baked with maybes. Maybes because she'd thought, I could not love Booey before, at least not completely, but now . . . maybe. Maybe. Maybe she could force herself onto this new Booey. Maybe this time Booey would choose her. Maybe. She made the cakes with devil spit too, because Mama would always say, "A nasty mouth no different than a nasty mind." And when her saliva sprayed on Booey's cakes, she was sure her head wasn't brimming with Jesus.

Ray Blake emerged from the black air. He was half-hidden by an oak furred with Spanish moss. He wore a cotton shirt and overalls, the evening heat forming dark spots underneath his armpits and around his planet-round belly. He came closer, rubbed the bristles on his chin, and wrinkled his nose.

"Yeah, I got some good cakes here. Can't have one. Sorry, Ray." Her eyes traveled to the package in her hands. Ray's face always made Sugar shiver a bit. Still, she felt a kinship with him. Booey had said of Ray: "He a man with a spirit of devils, a spirit of a beast."

Ray scratched his protruding breasts. "What you doing here, Red? Didn't your mama tell you to stay inside on account that I might getcha?" He curled his fingers and growled teasingly.

"That your fault, ain't it?" The girl grinned, unfolded her kerchief, and gave him a cake. Ray smiled and popped the food into his mouth.

"I like being here. It's peaceful—that tasted fine, by the way—and nobody want me killed. Can't even go to town to play cards now. Everybody want my head. They all say I fucked up Booey."

Red sucked her teeth, watching Ray's huge cheeks bounce up and down as he chewed. "You ain't helpin' yourself," she said. "Potato's trampin' the swamps like a watchdog. You hangin' 'round so close to Booey's house make it look like you houndin' her again."

He chuckled and wiped his mouth with three fingers. "Girl, first off, I ain't 'fraid of that skinny coon. Second off, your old sack of Black grandma is too crazy for me to negotiate with civil, so I don't see no point in talking to her."

Red smirked. "You weren't never civil. And if she dead, you better off."

Ray rushed up to the girl; seized her shoulder; ensnared her with his eyes—urine-colored things with little red, angry rivers. He spit: "I ain't no killer, girl. My dogs never meant no bad. They made a mistake. I ain't no . . . no wolf like Booey used to say I was. I sure as hell ain't blessed, but I ain't no beast."

"I don't think you bad, Ray Blake. I'm telling the truth,"

Red said. Ray released her arm and took a step backward. He studied the ground for a few moments, kicked a pebble into a bed of marshy brush. A muskrat slipped by his heels and ducked into a mash of drenched leaves. When he turned his head back to Red, his eyes were glistening. "Well, I ain't," he said, "but are you?"

Thea swallowed and retied the handkerchief holding her cakes. "You take care, Ray. Don't get back too late."

Ray pressed his lips into a grin. "I won't. Take care yourself, sweet girl. Sweet as sugar, Sugar Red. You a good child, got a good piece inside of you. Stay safe."

When Red pushed open Special House's rose-colored door and called, "Heyyy-o, Booeey! It's your grandbaby!" Booey didn't call back as she usually did:

"Come on in, Sugar Red!"

Regardless, Red knew Booey was somewhere in the place. The room smelled like Booey—it reeked of old oak, ash, and sweat. Red plodded into the living room and glanced around. The room was barren, save for the overstuffed pink armchair centered on the wooden floor, facing a gas fireplace. Just as Red thought, Booey was slumped in the seat, the folds underneath her chin spilling onto her collar like sloppy jelly. Red clenched her jaw and said nothing. Booey looked unreal. Crumbly. Her face was a mess of dirty skinfolds and whorls of loose wrinkles. Her snowdust hair was damp.

"Hey, Booey . . . ," she tried once more, smoothing her

braids, straightening her gingham skirt. Why was she fixing herself for a woman who didn't care about her? "Booey . . ."

Her neck snapped up. Red stumbled backward, stunned. Booey's eyes fixed on her granddaughter, her gaze yellow, hateful.

Red swore. She'd come to visit Booey during one of her spells. She shouldn't have come, shouldn't have made those damn cakes. No devil spit, no maybes.

"Ah! Hey! Don' be!" Booey cried out and leapt to her feet. Red didn't know what to do. Could she call for Ray, Potato? Weren't they outside now?

"Booey . . . I brought you somethin' nice . . . ," Red said. The old woman staggered over to her, her eyes shivering and wild.

"See 'em? Them dogs fixin' to get me, and they gonna get you too, devil gal!"

Right, Sugar Red shouldn't have come.

Booey threw her hands at Red's shoulders and thrust her back. Red caught herself on the doorframe to avoid falling through the open door. Booey shoved Red again, this time into the green evening air. A cicada chorus sang, "Haylo!"

Red slammed onto the porch and nearly slid to the end of the deck.

At first Sugar Red thought Booey would retreat into Special House, but she didn't. Instead, Booey joined Red, who was splayed on Special House's porch, clutching the white railing for her life. The old woman's limbs and arms and bones seemed colossal, her eyes blood-bright.

"They gonna get you first, you foul girl! And they shoulda, I say they shoulda!" Booey's mammoth breast rose and fell violently. In an instant the old woman was kneeling beside Red, fitting her fingers around the girl's neck.

"You can't see them dogs, baby? You don' see why they here?"

At this point Red experienced two things, her truths. One: She was not frightened at all of Booey. In fact, Red was enthralled by this madwoman. Her child-blood bubbled with excitement. This Booey was so wretched and evil the girl felt splendid, fine. She wanted Booey to slap her, kiss her on her cheeks, bludgeon her until she was unconscious. And two: Ray's ghost dogs were indeed alive (and kickin'!) and had indeed already consumed Ol' Booey. As Booey strengthened her grip and the air left Red's throat, she saw those beasts clearly. She saw two of them, black and heavily muscled, surging from her grandmother's balding scalp. Here they were! The devil dogs that tore through her brothers, the ones that gave the boys a crown of blood. The ones that ate up the last of Booey's old heart. Here they came!

Because of these two truths, Thea acted as she did. Even though the girl sensed, instinctively, she was going to die, she focused on other thoughts. Noble thoughts. Like how to save Booey. Ah, Poor Booey was possessed. Poor Booey needed to be free. The girl reached up and slashed the devil dogs in Booey's face with her nails. When that Ol' Mad Prophet stumbled back, disoriented, she let Thea go. The girl pounced on the dogs scampering all over Booey's ugly flesh. She hit the beasts with her fists until they stopped barking. Thea used a flowerpot to beat them, beat them, beat them. Their growls continued on for quite a while, so Thea bashed them until their mouths closed. After a good bit of time, their cries transformed into yelps of submission, and Satan yanked the animals back home. Red thought: Be gone, dead dogs!

The child stared at her grandmother's red arms and legs, stretched open on the floorboards. Like Jesus. Ol'Booey was still thinking she was Jesus. Red kissed Booey's brow and pushed the old woman's body the best a child can to the edge of the stairs. She gave her grandmother a final heave-ho.

"Hey, Booey! Hey, Grandmamma!" she said. "You didn't need them cakes! I freed you, and that's better. See now? I freed you, Booey! Y'aint need no town for that, nah? Right . . . now we're both okay!"

That Night, Thea would remember with a feeling.

Present:
Baton Rouge, Louisiana (1932)

A half hour passed and both Potato and Thea refused to speak. Potato played with his lips. He focused on this new woman trapped in a too-tight dress, her breasts puffing up over the top of the V-line. He focused on her profile, the severe shape of the frowning lips, the contrasting smooth lines of the chin. He focused on the brain he couldn't see, wondered if it were now remembering That Night as he had, remembering how he found little Red, how he brought her to his home, how he knew. How he knew the truth and she didn't know he did, how he didn't want to believe she had done such a thing, but he had seen her hands. He had walked the trail leading back and found that young girl cowering in blood and blackness. He had seen the broken flowerpot. He hated what he knew, the truth that nearly knocked him dead. And he still didn't know why she'd do it. Booey's sweet little girl.

Thea scratched her neck and leaned her forehead onto balled fists. Her heavy hair tumbled forth and obscured the left half of her face. "You think I'm being cruel to you? I know I am. I don't know. Potato, since you here now . . . can I ask you something . . . a few somethings?"

Potato stared forward. "Yeah-up. Go ahead."

"All right. Good. Okay . . ." Thea swallowed. "Are you the reason Ray died? Did you tell the town he killed Booey?"

Potato shrugged. "Yeah. I just told them what looked right."

"Jesus Christ." Thea looked up and closed her eyes. She opened them, stared at the distracted bartender. "Why you protect me?"

Potato chugged the air in his glass. Tasted like nothing, filling him with nothing. He ignored her question. "Ray probably had it coming. Probably did things in his life bad enough to die for."

"I don't know. I did things in my life bad enough to die for too."

"Maybe you did. I don't know," said Potato. "You were

little when it happened. Young people do bad things when they don't understand them."

"I weren't that little."

"That's right."

"Did you only save me because I was Booey's kin?" Thea said, near-desperately. "Did you only save me because you loved Booey?"

"I don't know," Potato said. "Of course, I loved Booey. I loved you too. You and her was so perfect to me. But I guess if I was really loyal to her, I would've handed you over."

"Why didn't you?"

"Jesus!" Potato slapped his knee. "I don't know. Didn't think I'd be forgiven if I handed over a babygirl to that town."

Thea closed her eyes. She scooted up on the barstool. "Forgiven by who? How you know Booey was really oh-so perfect? How you know I didn't do what I did to protect myself? How you know what happened when you wasn't there?"

"I don't know." Potato licked his lips. "That's too many questions."

"You don't know nothing."

"I don't." Potato slammed his palms on the tabletop. "Red, gal, nobody knows nothing! Nothing! You know what happened to you, I know what happened to me. Our goddamn town don't have to matter this much if you don't want it to. Look. Nobody left from Emmaus is talking about it. Fact is, we could say anything about the damn place and we'd be right. Think anyone would've known damn Jesus was the Son of God if he didn't have four fellas writing nice about him? Thea, you and I decide whether Emmaus need to live or die. We decide if we want a saint's name." Potato shook his head. The old man craned his neck to look about the bar, still frothing with vodkas, boogies, burning cigars, and zippers tearing down. He wondered how many years he had left before he would die.

Thea lifted her head from her fist. "Is that why you came to fetch me?"

"What?" Potato said, turning back to her.

"Did you come fetch me to make Emmaus live? That the only reason you came?"

Potato opened his mouth to say something perfect, then closed it. It was not as perfect as he thought. He decided on this: "Did you really hate us? Emmaus and Booey?"

Thea started sharply and, before he could continue, she slapped Potato across the cheek. Hard. He swayed back and forth, his eyes rolling about. After he recovered, Potato grabbed Thea's shoulders and growled:

"What the fuck's wrong with you, girl?"

Red flexed her biceps. "You know me. You just like me. You got that demon in you too. With all your making an innocent man guilty, with all your lies. Even if you did 'em for me, they lies, lies, lies. See? Booey's goodness was lies, lies, lies."

Potato let the girl go and blew loud air through his nostrils. Thea glared at him, jumped from her seat, snatched her purse from her side. At first Potato thought she would stomp away or nail him in the face with the golden bag. Instead, the girl unzipped her purse and took out a piece of paper. She started to thrust it into Potato's hands but reconsidered upon remembering the old man could not read. Thea held her paper to eye level, swallowed, and read aloud with the precision of one who knows few words but prizes each letter:

"Emmaus, Louisiana. Between 1865 and 1923 home to eight hundred to eleven hundred residents. Colored population: 89 percent. Founder: Claude Freedman, former Republican delegate. Land grant: 1869. Landmark: 'Special House.' Current status of Emmaus: Disused."

"What's that?" Potato said.

Thea folded the paper and placed it back in her purse. "I'm answerin' your question. The Negro in the Blue Suit found that for me in the papers 'cause I mentioned where I came from, just once. He said he wanted to know about Negroes; he said he liked hearing there were places where Negroes lived tucked away. He read the rest of the article out loud to me and it had words about Emmaus like 'de-pray-ved,' which means 'bad,' and 'im-puch-ooh-nee-us,' which means 'don't got nothing.' He didn't like that, and neither did I. See, Potato, the story didn't say nothing about the spirits inside of folks, nothing about my Booey, nothing about the roads and sweetbread and Mama and Ray. Nothing about what I did—" Her voice cracked but she recovered quickly. "Nobody gave a damn. I don't know what to do with Emmaus. It's sticky. If it stays inside of me too long, it feels . . . like a baby that need to get out. And that feel so sad inside, but Jesus, I can't . . . how do I? I can't . . . let it . . ."

She flung her head back to keep the water in her eye-ducts, aware she was still in Sweet Heaven. She couldn't weep in a place like this. Here the men expected caramel-sweet words and intimations of nights with a caramel lady's legs wide open. They didn't want crying little country girls. Potato watched her, with that mucus dribbling from her nose to her lips, mascara streaking dark, ragged lines down her cheeks. She looked very much like a little girl. But Potato liked this face, liked it immensely. This girl, his town's Sugar Red grown up, was a breathtaking mess. If he weren't so tired, he'd find a place to cry too. If he didn't have so many useless, imperfect answers, he'd laugh.

Potato came to his feet. "I'm going. You comin' along?"

Thea said, "*You* ready, Potato?"

"I'm good," Potato said. "Holy-good. Feelin' like a prophet, somebody like that."

Thea wiped her face with the back of her hand and smiled. She glanced at the men at the bar then back at the skinny goat whose head resembled a potato.

"Let's get out of here. Go someplace new. We'll decide what to do when we get there."

Potato nodded.

La Espera

Sofi

IVETTA AND I ARE WEARING NEW DRESSES. MAMI-
made. We are wearing them for Papi, because Mami wants
us to look pretty for him when he comes back to Villa del
Carmen from New York, which will be very soon. Three
hours, maybe a little bit longer. Mami told us: *let's impress him
with your loveliness.*

My sister and I are twins. We are twelve years old and
we share the same berry-black faces. Most people can tell us
apart, though, since I have a birthmark on my cheek in the
shape of a hibiscus leaf and my family remembers me as the
one with the defect. Mami says our twoness was a surprise to
Papi. She says a few days after we were born, he started a little
garden behind Mami's one-room house. El jardín para tus

gemelitas. When Mami bought the fabric for the dresses we wear today, she told us to pick colors that would remind Papi of his favorite flowers. We wear his flor-colored dresses now. Ivie is in orchid-white, I am in rosselle-purple, the color of the flor de magas in Papi's garden. We pinch the new cloth, and it feels cold and smooth and smells like sweet kola nuts.

We are stuck hip-to-hip on Mami's couch in the parlor. Our ankles are crossed tight but quivery. Mami is retying our hair bows and licking her thumb then rubbing that thumb against our eyebrows. She's patting our faces and telling us to practice our smiles. Stretch them wide, she says, but not too wide. Bite your lips so they flush. We obey. We clean our teeth with our tongues. Ivetta and I grin, together. We stretch our smiles so wide our face-skin stings. I can feel my birthmark stretch and hurt.

Mami says: "He'll have to come, to see such beautiful girls."

We believe we look pretty in these dresses, like Mami tells us. Still, our fingertips and palms are sweat-wet. We haven't seen Papi in a month; we are used to not seeing him. He doesn't come to our house on Villa del Carmen much, and he has never been to our school plays or piano shows or seen us ride our glittery Huffys down Ponce calles. Sometimes, the night before Papi is scheduled to fly in, Ivie and I lay awake, shivering in the bed we share together. We hug each other's waists, try to sleep, and murmur about the same kinds of things: What happens if Papi stops coming to see us? What if he decides we're not worth his time? We wonder if there will be a day when we're not beautiful enough to make Papi come back.

Mami says we are the first reason Papi comes to Puerto Rico. We think Mami is the second, but when we ask her about this, she waves her hands and scowls.

When Papi comes, he always comes with boxes. Hatboxes for Mami, glossy-faced dolls from the States that have negra noses and lips, that look like us. When Papi comes, he'll kiss our heads and laugh at our yowls of delight when we tear open our gift boxes. The living room will get fat with light and the walls will glow yellow. Mami will lean her chest against Papi's long body and he'll stroke her wig. She'll kiss his chin, he'll half smile, and we'll be like the children in school who have parents in love, or parents who are not in love but have electric hips smashed together at dinner parties. When Papi comes, looks at us, and says que niñas lindas, we feel like treasures.

Mami doesn't look like normal-Mami today, but she is still beautiful. Mami's black-brown curls are usually cut above her ear, but today, she puts on hair that is long and honey colored and loose and falls right above her chest. She wears pink lipstick and bright red blush, and her skin is doll-smooth and shining like the face of an ocean pebble. She has high shoes with a tall heel, like the girls Abuela warns us about from Santurce. Mami wears a necklace Papi bought for her, strung-together coral beads, a goose feather, a bright rock he got from a vendor in Vieques. Mami's dress is white and flimsy looking and fits tight against her body, like a new, special skin. Mami's real skin, the color of the earth where the coquis skitter, is lotion-rubbed. After she fixes our hair, again and again, she walks in a circle around the couch.

"What do you think Papi will bring us?" Ivetta asks me as she watches Mami pace.

"I don't know," I say. "It'll be good."

"Maybe we'll go to La Parguera," Ivetta says. She is tugging on her left braid. "We'll bring piraguas to the top."

"No. The piraguas will melt. Too sticky, and I'll touch Papi's arm with my sticky hands and he'll yell at me," I tell her. Papi likes us washed and unmessy. He says girls like us must be extra clean.

"We'll take pictures," she goes on. She scratches her plaits hard. "We look so good. I want him to remember how good we look today."

"No fotos," I say. I think about the birthmark in the shape of a flower on my cheek. About how terrible it looks on camera. I am afraid Papi will look at the pictures when he's in the States and think I'm the one he should leave behind when he finally takes us to the U.S. I have tried to cover up the birthmark with Mami's makeup, but it never works.

"I'll ask him for something you can only get in New York. Something very caro," Ivetta says. "Then we can brag to the kids in class, like those San Juaneros in second period always do." She fingers the braid until the tight hair comes loose.

"Let's not," I say. Ivie and I have never been to the States, but I can't imagine it's all that special. We already learn English in school and all the malls have States-stores and we see enough States-made shows on television every day. San Juan and Ponce move fast enough; that's what Papi says. Don't be around bright lights or too many people, and you will be much happier, Papi also says.

Mami snaps at Ivetta, tells her to stop touching her hair, says she's not greasing it again. She walks back over to us, and her hips jut up and down. The tops of her small breasts are shining and bouncing with each step. She fluffs my bangs. She makes the flor de maga above my hair clip fit snug. She reties Ivetta's braid and sighs into her face.

Mami steps back, looks us over. She says, "This is how he should see you."

She turns around and stands in front of a wall clock. It is 4:23. Papi is supposed to arrive from New York at seven o'clock. Maybe eight thirty if Mami's friend Rico gets stuck in traffic coming from the other side of the island. Mami walks around in a half circle. She puts her hands on her hips, hips that puff out wide from her waist. She readjusts her wig and licks her lips wet.

"Don't expect anything," Mami says. She is swallowing hard. She is making our hair clips look right. "Don't think about what he will do."

Camila

I am watching my girls shiver on the couch. One. Two. My girls are bright-faced and brown, like me, with Carlos's feathery curls. They are mine, always. They sometimes belong to him.

When I first called Carlos about the birth of my twingirls, told him my stomach was filling up with his babies; he wouldn't hear me. I heard him cough, in a room I'd never seen, somewhere on the Upper East Side, in New York City. He told me I shouldn't be such a lying puta, that the neighbor Rico always liked me, and that Rico had probably come over some night. Carlos thought then, maybe, I wanted his lawyer money. I cussed him out and told him I hated him, and Carlos said the same and then called back later and said he'd come back to Puerto Rico to teach me some kind of lesson. And he came, the month after the call. He remembered I was good to him, and we hiked the Peñón, watched dusk crumble to nightfall, and he told me what must be done to my insides. I told him no, but he offered me more money than I'd seen in half of my life. I took his Special Lawyer money, went sailing in the Keys alone, and gave the rest to my father's restaurant. Then I gave my twingirls life, on the island. I wouldn't let Carlos snuff out his secrets that easily.

Carlos didn't see me again until a week after I'd had the twins. He saw our gemelas in my arms, little and red and looking like both of us, and he loved them quickly. The bigger they grew, the more Carlos remembered how much he loved me, how I was the sort of woman who made him laugh, who he remembered was fizzy like a freshly opened soda can. He described his apartment on the Upper East Side and said we could all live together and we'd have hot caffe lattes in the morning at Russ & Daughters. That we'd all stroll, me, Carlos, and the twins, with hands clutched over the green humps and swells of Central Park. Because of these promises, ugly hope filled me daily. I knew he was lying. I wasn't sure if I loved him, sometimes, but I wanted my children to have these rich fantasies. I wanted to be free of his red strings, wanted that for my sister too. He'd say, "You already are free, amor, that's why I like you," to further hook me. A cruel thing to say. He'd say he was forced to marry my sister because of our father's request to him when we were young, but that he'd always loved me first. What Carlos told me: I made him weak and soupy. He'd rather feel weak; that's what love was about. That's what that puto said. He successfully severed bonds between me and my sister, who I can no longer love in full. And yet, I fell into this mess.

I am watching my girls and know that Carlos's shark-mouth smile, that collection of many-sized teeth, is much bigger and more powerful when he sees these little ones. He has gone back to leaving us for months at a time, but this time he called and gave a date and time. He says he will come. I believe him, and I shouldn't.

Now, I am looking at the clock and I am pacing again. The girls are happy-nervous and talking about expectations. How Papi will take them to the mountains and put them on his hard shoulders so they can see the way the sun pinkens over turtle grass, allergena trees, and ink-colored hills of homes. That he'll swing them around in circles. I'll take their pictures on Carlos's phone. Of him and them, me and them. Then Carlos will take a picture of just me. He and I will not take a picture together. He will keep these pictures secret and never show anyone, but I know he'll look at them in the middle of the night when my sister is snoring next to him.

Now, the girls are talking about Papi's gifts, and I hush them. They talk about Americano films and baby dolls and trinkets from the States, but I know them, and I know they are like me, focusing on easy things you can hold. Gifts. Gifts are things that last when their father is gone. They are real and they are proof that Carlos was once there.

I know they are nervous with love for him. I tell myself I simply want them to have a Papi. I want them to remember the quivery lines on their Papi's face. I don't want them to have the father that my sister and I had, a stranger whose face looked new every time we saw him. I tell myself I have my pride and it's been fourteen years of loving him in snatched-up moments on my island, with clasped hands nobody can see. I can count the gray hairs sprouting from my crinkly roots. Sometimes I get strong inside and tell myself things: that I am a new, firm-faced woman who will live to care for her children. I tell myself that I am going to crawl out of the Carlos-hole and live a fine life, but I can feel the pulse of the lie. The truth is: Carlos is terrible, but

I am trapped. It's a wolf of a feeling, whatever it is, and it's not pure love. It's fanged and grisly; it's been gobbling me up for so long I think the pain has always been with me, like a little mole on my right thumb or the mark on Sofi's face. The other women on Villa have known Carlos as long as me, since we were all young and in Catholic school and praying to that Big Blanco Señor. Since Carlos and I worked the night shifts at my father's restaurant downtown. Since Carlos gave up waiting tables for New York law and I stayed in Puerto Rico to work at the local nursery school. His and my family excuse Carlos's behavior, say I should know better, that Carlos is traditional and traditional Puerto Rican men are like this, so no me importa. Everything is my problem and I am the puta of a street with few negras. The women of our pueblo know my girls, and love them sometimes, but they laugh at me. We know Carlos is the sort to stray, they say, we can't hate him for being the way he is. A handsome Boricua man with that kind of money and that kind of face. What do you expect? Of course, he has many women. Be thankful for those girls. You, mija, are the moyeta waiting for him, you are the one who cleaves that which is holy. I have fallen into this mold.

I remind myself that at least I had a choice in waiting for Carlos. I don't want to be that kind of negra who hates my own blood, my own women, white or otherwise, because of a man. I am not like that. I am better than that. But I am also a person who is in pain. I remind myself that there was once a time in which there was no Carlos, and my sister and I would

smile and salsa and love, before we both fell into nasty feelings and our parents meddled with our lives. That in another
life, my sister and I could be family again, purely. There is
still a simmering of love between us. We are a man away from
being together. I remind myself that a feeling is just that. An
invisible push that makes a woman soft inside. What is real: I
have a good job that makes money, and the dress I am wearing today, white, ill-fitting, is a dress I bought for myself, and
not just so Carlos will remember what he loves. The dress is
mine. But still, I have things inside I don't know how to fix.
Still, I have these girls.

I am watching these girls and I walk over and make
them prettier with my hands and the spit on my fingers. I
see them and me and him: his butter-brown skin and my
heart-shaped lips. When I see them, pretty-looking, I know
at least Carlos will gaze upon them and remember the children I gave him, that these two faces could only have been
created from our fierce fighting and stupid, abstract bond.
When I see those faces, when I see Sofi, my girl with her
birthmark and my twitching mouth, I see the best kind of
beautiful.

My girl with the birthmark says, "Mami. Can I use your
makeup for a moment? I want to fix my face like yours."

I look at the girl who looks different and know that everyone will remember her as such, for the rest of her life. My
Sofi, who will always be compared to my other lovely girl,
unfavorably.

I think about turning on the television to drown out the

sound of the air conditioner, which is the sound of itchy silence, which is the sound of fear. Instead, I walk over to the
bookshelf. I toss a book with Albizu's face on the cover, a
biography I read as a teen, on Sofi's lap. Sofi ruffles her brow,
stares at its finger-smudged face. She doesn't touch it. I say,
"See how I used to be smart and free? Put something in your
head so you don't end up like your mami," and those words
come out mean.

Elena

It is August in New York, and the sun is a beast. It growls
and bangs through the window above the basin and sinks its
sharp-tipped canines into our apartment kitchen. It is 12:00
p.m. and I am making pechuga de pollo and arroz con gandules with my homemade sofrito for my husband. Carlos is
supposed to eat my food but there is a good chance he will
skip my meals, because he won't be hungry at noon. He'll
eat bullshit American staples at the airport. There is a good
chance he'll get something quick, on his way to catch a plane
to San Juan, to see, and fuck, my little sister.

The broken air conditioner bothers me. I am sweating.
Every day my pits smell bad from my sweating about something. Carlos. Where our money goes, why Carlos has locked
the accounts from me. My future, my past.

I wipe my face with a checkered dishrag, and I pull my
hair back into a dark ponytail that goes limp immediately

after it's tied. I resolve to get that air conditioner fixed this week. I lean over the sink and my ponytail falls over my shoulder and I see it, and how mousy it looks in the summer light. I frown. I'm thinking if Carlos leaves today, this will be the last sign. I will leave New York, go to D.C., Boston, or even new cities in Puerto Rico—I'll go to some fresh place with people I barely know. I'll go where I can be reborn. I have been saving enough money for myself, money Carlos never sees and can never use on my sister or her children. I will move in with my friends in Queens for a month or two. Then, I'll leave. I'll start again. Maybe, in the meantime, I could call the air conditioning man, who says I am a quick thinker. I have no children, unlike my sister; I am a man away from being free. If Carlos leaves today, there are all sorts of better places I could go.

Carlos says he's catching a plane to Puerto Rico late in the day, that he has made plans. He needs to see his family in San Juan. He never names which family members. I am supposed to assume his mami, who hates me, but I am not supposed to ask. Carlos and I grew up on Villa de Carmen—where everyone knows everyone—and when I heard from friends, a year after we were married, that Carlos would frequently show up in Ponce instead of staying in the city, I suspected he might not be seeing his mami in San Juan all that much. You see, men like Carlos are wedded to their mamis and their mamis control them. Still, faithful Bori-merican boys might visit the island to please their mamis for a weekend or so, but they'll always come back to love their second esposa, for sex and comida, at the very least. After three weeks, though, their mami would have let them go, because this old-school mami would have deferred, in this time, to son-love. She'd say: son knows best. So what would keep my Carlos in our hometown so long that often, without a stir? No question. My sister.

I told my own mami what I suspected before the children were born. Mami is not good at lying, but she likes stories. When I told her about Carlos and Camila, she just laughed and said, "Oh, probably. He always liked her. What can you do? She is my child too and I love her too." Then, she said, "You are his wife, mija. As I was wife to your dog father, regardless of what he did. You are Carlos's first, no matter who he loves." I told her, in fear, that that wasn't enough. That I loved Carlos, but I wanted him to remember his vows and shake off his obsession. That I was bound by a ring. Mami said, "Yes, and you can't take that off. He is our family pa'siempre. You will be fine. Your sister isn't the sort to be serious about marriage. She's all about passion. You are different. Eres buena."

I'm not buena nor different. And Camila wasn't very passionate growing up; she was like me, careful. We dreamed of liberation before we met Carlos and planned our lives as free women. Now Carlos has given us poison. If I were buena, I wouldn't pray for Carlos to get bored with Camila, even though she has his children, who need him more than me. I wouldn't feel a rush of nasty joy when Carlos came back to me after his "family trips" on the island. That he'd tell me I was his first choice and Camila would always be his "maybe" or "sometimes." These feelings were not what Camila and I dreamed about when we talked about escaping our family, starting anew in San Juan, becoming liberated women.

Still. When Carlos told me he was leaving this morning, I begged him to stay in New York with me. I told him I would pay for the missed-flight fee with my own money. I wanted him to be here when the air conditioner got fixed. I told him I wanted him to talk to the man who showed up because when I'm alone in this place on the Upper East Side, a place I've never been fond of, I don't feel comfortable. The last man who showed up to fix the AC was my landlord's middle-aged son, who I called for help often, who was handsome. He showed up with his birch-colored hair slicked back and plaid shirt tight and halfway unbuttoned. He wasn't dressed to fix a thing. I was dressed like a wife at home, who rarely left the apartment but to cross the street and walk the hills of Central Park. The landlord's son thought my sweat and hair were sexy, and he pushed his thin chest close to my breast when he talked. I had to get that man out of the room when he started asking if I wanted children and whether or not Carlos was a good husband, and I lied about the last thing and said yes and ignored the first because the first thing stung. I pushed him out of Carlos's place, and he lingered at the door, not talking about the air conditioner or the pipes. He looked at me long, those eyes wide and stuffed with brown lines, and I thought it would be nice if his unshaved face bristled against my chin. He looked at me, then, like I was a pretty thing who could be special, but I pushed him out.

Now, I prefer Carlos to be home when work gets done to the house. I prefer for him to stay with me in the evenings and not leave me when he gets time off, to go to these firm "meetings" or to see his mami, because I know about these meetings and some of them are real and many of them are to see my sister in Ponce and "their" children. He thinks I don't know about him or my own sister. That the old biddies in town don't talk and haven't told me close to everything. That those biddies hope I hate my hermana. I could, easily, if I wanted to. She might hate me too. But I know we still love each other, somehow.

I leave the kitchen and go into the bedroom. Carlos is lying in our queen bed, with his shirt off, coiled black curls coating his pectorals. Our room is stuffed with a fat kind of hot, the sort that crowds me. Carlos's hands are pressed flat against his chest, and he is staring at the ceiling. Our pink sheets clutch his ankles, and I can see the soft brown paunch, layered with crisscrossed hairs, resting above his boxers. That paunch is small enough that nobody notices it when he stands up. That fat looks kind and cuddly when I love him. When I feel like he loves me, I like to bury my face in that warm belly. That belly looks taunting when I'm angry at him, a sign he can forget things that have always been attached to him. I don't know how I feel about his stomach today.

I say, "Tienes hambre?" and his head flops over. His eyes sweep my body. I am wondering if he sees the fleshy places around my arms or the paunch I have above my jean buckle. I wonder if he is judging me, weighing me against my sister. It would always be easy for Camila to be hated; she is dark and different; she would always destroy the fabric of family. It doesn't take much for them to push her out if need be. I used to sympathize; she was my sister. But then Carlos came, and I lost my ability to remember the things I read in my favorite books. I became insecure. I fight the Carlos-poison. I do.

Because I know all that matters to Carlos is him. Him mattering. My mami wants me to stay with Carlos. Carlos's mami hates me. I can't love my sister in full, and she can't love me. There is no winning for us women.

I could hate Carlos and his flesh if I wanted to, today. I want to.

I rearrange my clothes and ask my husband if he is hungry again. I tell him about the food, and he looks up and says, "You hate me. I am bad."

I tell him, no. I don't think he is bad. I think he is pathetic, but I don't say so. He looks at the rippled bumps on our ceiling and says, "I want to go. You hate me for wanting to go."

I say, "To the island," and I mean my sister. The word comes out sharp. His eyes flash at me, fast. Ponce, my sister, they have never been words that feel like they belong to me. I look more like my Corsican father. Olive skin, long, sleek dark hair. My mother, a negra from San Juan, looks like my sister, who is black-skinned. I was called prettiest for most of my life, for useless reasons that have something to do with a hierarchy of Puerto Rican colors that I'm not interested in. My bright skin can't make my husband love only me, and it didn't stop the accident from marring my leg. Now, Carlos has aged me. My sister has aged too, but it wouldn't matter who looked like what, at any point, now. I have been loved, sometimes, but never enough to make Carlos stay in New York, for me. She has been loved, sometimes, too. Nothing is enough for him.

Carlos shakes his head.

"It is very hard to live here. In this city," he tells the ceiling.

We are not talking about New York.

I go over to the sofa chair and pick up his jeans and shirt.

"The city is difficult," I say. "But when you first got to New York, you loved it. You made such a big deal about it. It was everything San Juan wasn't."

"It's tiresome. Too busy. It drains me. I was wrong."

"New York is a familiar kind of exciting. Now all you see is the gray and all you see is the sludge and all you see is the way people push each other when they try to get along." I am running my hand through my hair, and I pinch the roots of my forehead, which are gray.

I walk around the length of the bed, still holding his clothes. "There is always a better place for you to go. If you went to Mayagüez or back to Ponce, you would think about New York. Or L.A. or Chicago. You always want to go to a new place. Mallorca. Barcelona. Berlin. Paris. Tokyo. Who knows! Do you want to be that kind of man? Who never feels secure anywhere? Who can never be fine with things, or people, that are just okay?"

Carlos turns his head to me. I didn't expect to see his face. His eyes get wet; the wrinkles around his mouth deepen.

"Puñeta. Why am I like this? Will you help me?"

Carlos stares at me, his wife, standing in front of the television, holding his dirty clothes.

"Te adoro . . . I love you . . ." He starts to say something else, but I gesture at his laundry and spit, "Put your dirty clothes in the wash."

I don't want to hear his love-words. They feel used up. I know he has kissed them into my sister's neck and that he has brushed her hair back, and imagining this kind of love has made me hate my own blood-kin, and her little brown children who I cannot know but would like to love. His words make me hate the man who gave me a little silver band he and my mami won't let me take off. I can't live a life of hating people I'm supposed to love. Over this man who loves nobody.

There is a long silence. Carlos is still staring at me, and his eyes make the right side of my face weaken, and then those weak feelings push into my cheek-skin and beyond and then I feel, inside, he does love me. I feel a surge of wild longing and reassurance and hope. I turn back to him and lick my lips, and I am about to respond, but then his eyes get dim. He rethinks something I can't see him rethinking.

"But there are things down there I need to take care of. I have a garden. I have ventures."

"It can be taken care of by someone else," I say, wondering why I bother with his excuses. "What ventures?"

"I want to see the garden," he half whines, and of course we are not talking about the garden, not anything now. And because we are not talking about the garden, because we are talking about the Black children who are not mine and who I cannot give to him because my womb is like Leah's or Sarah's or another timeless wife's, I say nothing and leave the room. I don't want to be the kind of blanca woman who hates Black women, my own blood, out of spite and jealousy. Not over Carlos, or any man. I am better than this. Still, I am a person who is in pain.

I return to the kitchen, and it is hotter than before. The heat is peeling my skin off.

I yell at the kitchen window, "Carlos, you bought the plane ticket. You're going today." It's not a question. I know the answer already.

I hear nothing. I hear the croak of the bed as he gets up. He sounds like a tired man spitting out something too big for his mouth. I know what he will do.

Carlos

Oye, I'll tell you: I have a timeless story and it is boring and terrible. This is the story, and it surprises no one. A man finds a good woman, then he finds another. He keeps them both because he is selfish and cowardly. The man discovers love is a thing that can spray like hose water, and this timeless man doesn't know how to turn off his own fucking hose.

I am lying on the bed, and I know the fucking time. The plane is supposed to leave at three and land at six; then Rico, Camila's friend, is supposed to take me from San Juan to Ponce. It is 12:30 p.m. and I am in bed, in my apartment on the Upper East Side. I do not know if I will get a taxi to LaGuardia or take the subway to get on the plane. Elena, who is soft-skinned and steady, and loves me without inflicting trouble or strife, is in our kitchen. She is cleaning our place, which is ours, which I paid for, but she deserves. Camila is waiting for me with my children. My black gemelas who share my face and are born of my love for Camila, my first crush, the woman I should have just left alone.

Elena comes in. She doesn't look at me. I watch her thin body reach and move and stretch. She is such a sturdy woman, despite her small size and slight weight. She is so capable and powerful in her littleness. I get pissed at myself for not loving her more, even though she bores me. I am beginning to find everything, in all life, boring, and this is the worst place to be.

While I'm pissed and watching my wife, Camila's face

burns back in. I see the hard angles of her face, the dancer-slopes of her tall body; I imagine her tiny, snowcap-shaped breasts. I'd worked as a waiter at Camila and Elena's father's restaurant before I started teaching at Escuela Intermedia in my early twenties, before I saved up and went to law school. Camila had been a waitress at her father's spot, and I fell in love with her first and fast. She was a little cold and rarely smiled, but when she did, she made me feel hot-faced. Her sister, Elena, was prim and proper and gave up smiles freely and easily. She'd be a good wife, visually and mannerism-wise, but I wasn't interested in getting married. I wanted to have young fun with someone and let love develop, genuinely, over time. Elena would come in and clean the tables, with all those perfected smiles, but she, like Camila, was good at ignoring me. After half a year of playing push-and-pull games with Camila, I finally convinced her to go out on a date with me, and for the whole date she rebuffed every wink, side-glance, or offer. We went salsa dancing and got drunk, but she stayed a safe distance from me. Whenever I got close to her hot mouth, she'd pull away or turn. I remembered moving her hair, huge and floppy then, away from her ear, and whispering to her: "Why are you so far away from me?" She finally said, midway through some Chick Corea cut, "My sister likes you." And I said, "Bueno. But you came with me today." She said, "I know. But I love my sister more than you. And I know who you will choose." She hesitated. I got in close and tried to kiss her, and she ran off. That night I jacked off to her until I fell asleep and woke up hungover and angry at Elena for no other reason than she was the obstacle from me getting the girl I wanted. Of course, the challenge made me more interested in Camila.

The next day, Camila didn't come to work, and Elena walked in, looking for her. She looked me in the eye and said, "You went out with her last night." I said, "Yeah, sí." Her eyes, chocolate-colored, flitted away from me. I didn't feel as upset at Elena anymore, then. It felt lovely to have a girl like me, especially after all of Camila's rejection, even if I didn't share her feelings. Plus, I liked knowing Camila would be pissed if I hooked up with her sister. It felt like a little revenge, while that makes little sense. "Camila's nothing," I lied. I was a silly, insecure kid who wanted admiration from women. Perhaps if I'd said something different, the course of my messy life might have changed, but I said the thing, and now I have lived my mistake.

Elena looked confused after I told her Camila meant nothing to me. She tried to fight her face from smiling, but I saw her lips curl up, and that was enough. I could have continued on with my life, but then I told Elena she was pretty, because she was. Then I said some other things, like, "You are the reason I don't move to San Juan, seeing your face gives me purpose," or something like that, and it worked well. Before I knew it, Elena was smiling so big and I was smiling so big that I felt great about myself, almost like I had enough confidence to go back and try again with

Camila. But I didn't. I chickened out. Kept going out with Elena, until Camila eventually lost complete interest and before I knew it I was locked into a relationship I didn't really want to begin with, with a girl I'd grown platonically fond of, who was easy to talk to, cleaned well, and pumped up my ego when I felt like a wayward waiter with no future. Then, one night, we were driving back from a bar on Benigno Dávila, and an island shrew popped out of a cluster of swampy bushes. I swerved out of the way and hit a ceiba tree hard. Elena tore her upper leg during the accident. Got a scar that, to this day, hasn't left her thigh. I still have a long tear on my right palm too, but nobody notices it. Her father, the ever-traditionalist despite the coterie of women I saw him bang every week, brought me to his house. This old man said, after all I'd done, I should at least see his Elena seriously. Maybe marry her, at least marry her, since I'd been putting their family through so much strife. That old man thought I'd marred her too, that men couldn't love her anymore, because of me. Certainly bullshit. But blinded by shame and directionless, I proposed impulsively, and Elena said yes. Puñeta, right? I spent the next few years in despair and regret, until Camila rung me up and said, "I'm sick of seeing your twisted-up face around town. Get some money, cabrón. Get off the island, do something new," and I followed her advice. Took the LSATs, applied to law school in New York, and got in based off my impressive undergraduate record at UPRRP. I left the island with Elena, was too much of a coward to divorce her since she supported me brilliantly in law school. I passed the bar, got a job at a firm in Lower Manhattan, engaged in a long series of boring affairs in New York that filled me with more self-loathing and a guilty dick. Eventually, on one trip back to Puerto Rico, I went to see Camila, who was teaching at nursery school then, and invited her to dinner. At some domplin restaurant, I told her everything, that I didn't love Elena, that I'd always loved her and the only thing in my life that was stable was my career, that I'd never stopped thinking about her, that she'd saved me. Something like that. She was angry at me, immediately, and threw her butter knife at my face, which I dodged. To calm her down, I took her to Emajagua and we stared at the waves' pleat and pull. I kissed her and she was mad about it, but eventually she kissed me back, and I was, as ridiculous as it sounds to use this word: happy. Her defenses were down, then, and I, like a fool, continued to pursue her, selfishly and blindly, so ecstatic I'd finally found some kind of happiness but also terrified I'd embarrass Elena, lose her when I needed her normal love. I acted like a teen kid, even though I was a full-grown man, and my relationship with Camila dragged on and on, until the twins came, and then it lasted longer, until I became the sort of man who lies often, always, until the lies became my life and I grew numb to them, acquiescent to the idea that I was a shitty person who would never be fulfilled. That I was too cowardly to make choices without two kind, sharp-minded women to support me.

Now, I am under hard sheets. Elena has tucked me in mean. If you were to see me from afar, you'd see a boring, middle-aged tonto trapped in his own bed, a bed his wife has made perfectly around him. I reach for the top sheet. I pull it and it comes off easily, the second one does too, and I climb out of bed and stand up, in the apartment I have bought for both of us, but really just for me.

Elena is gone. She is in the kitchen, or somewhere I can't see. I leave my room and look at the hallways of my apartment. There are bedrooms and hardwood floors and picture frames, evidence of a series of life choices that were reversible and were not reversed but that have left me at one point, now, in which I have this apartment, a good career, and, undeservedly, two women and children who yearn for and depend on me. Is that some kind of power? Men love this kind of power. To have so many people hoping for, wanting, needing you. Do I? I can't tell.

I go to the bathroom. I look in the mirror, grab a comb, and slick my hair back. My skin is gray; I look too old for a man in his midforties. I see my face, the ragged lines under inky eyes. I'm sort of crinkly-looking; I have a high widow's peak. I'm in variously changing shape. I'm a fast talker, and I may have good money and degrees, but these women who have been with me my whole life aren't impressed with my money or anything flashy I might have.

This is not power.

I told Camila I would see her today. The plane will leave in a few hours. I told Elena some lie I barely remember. There are two little negra girls waiting for me that have my features. I can see them in my mind's eye. One has a birthmark, though they have the same face. The other is next to her, smooth-skinned and blank-eyed. They will both grow up and get hurt by people like me. There is a woman in that house, who I have always loved, perhaps, but cannot keep, because I am afraid of her. If I leave Elena to be with my first crush, Camila will eventually see me for all I am and reject me, in full. This is a terrible thing to think, and I think it often. Or worse, she will become boring like Elena. Pero oye, all of these women and girls. They do not belong to me; I cannot choose them as if I have the power to choose. My life has tangled into theirs; I have fooled us all into thinking I am in control, when we are all waiting for something indefinable that perhaps will never come.

The little girls who look like the first woman I've loved want to see me. I would like to know them more. When? Now? These children, who I should learn to love, I should show them what a man looks like. I should see what their kind of waiting looks like.

Mami told me everyone can be free if they tell the truth. She says this every time I see her, when she looks me in the eye, knowing everything. I look at her, my body full of throbbing lies and childishness that, like a palm or thigh scar, has never healed.

I am supposed to see Camila today.

I walk into the kitchen, to tell Elena, the woman who

I have married and not loved, who I have trapped in a little prison, what she needs to know.

This is a timeless story.

Sofi

The late-night dark has come, and the windows are purple. The coquis are shrieking; their song goes soft. I am still on the couch and my braids have come undone. Ivetta and I are wearing new dresses. Mami-made. We are wearing them for Papi, because Mami wants us to look pretty for him when he comes back to Villa del Carmen from New York, which will probably not happen.

When I whisper to Ivie that the windows have turned violet and the hot has grown and the late night is coming, she doesn't believe me. She thinks Papi is coming for sure.

Still, Mami has been in the kitchen for an hour on the phone. Sometimes she yells and sometimes she cries and sometimes her voice sounds like a little animal moaning after it's been hit by a city guagua. I check on her, see her heels flicking and snapping in a circle on the kitchen floor. I see her in that tight dress, her cell phone pressed close to her face. I wonder how Papi would look upon her, in that sexy-lady dress, if he would think it was too much. I don't know how men see women. I don't know what she could have done better.

I wonder why I care about a man who doesn't want to remember us.

Ivie stays on the couch. Her dress, the armpit part, is dark with sweat. She twists around to look out the window. She tugs her braid until it comes loose, and nobody fixes it. I come back to the couch and sit next to Ivie. I can still hear the clattering of Mami's high heels, as if the sound is blaring from a stereo on high. I hear Mami's voice get little, and I hear another lady-voice, and I wonder who this other woman could be. These voices get quiet. Mami and the mystery woman keep talking, their voices are even-leveled, without the sound of my papi. I detect some kind of love.

When Mami walks out of the kitchen, shoeless, her wig has been ripped off, and she has removed the cap, and all I see is her braids. She unwinds each plait slowly, in front of us, so we can see her work. After she is done, big curls spring forth. We three look at each other, not talking. We are all frizzy-haired too; the humidity has worn out the grease keeping our coils down. Mami's face is warm; she scrubs her makeup off. Her dark skin shines like Yemaya rising from water and this is the most beautiful I've seen her, even more than this morning.

She smiles at me and Ivie. Ivie is asking her about Papi, about what he will do, and Mami shrugs. She tells us he will not come this time and that he might come another time, but it doesn't matter if he does. She sits down next to us and holds us, her twingirls. In this heat and in Mami's arms, Ivie and I sigh together. We three breathe loud, as the night turns from purple to black. We don't know what time it is when we fall asleep or wake up, because we don't care. We aren't waiting for anything important.

Liberation Day

WHEN ESTELLE DECIDED TO LEAVE THE SISTERS OF Grace for good, she had no regrets. She'd already made the preparations before deciding to slip away. She'd passed two years of candidacy, made it to the novitiate phase. She still had her apostolic year to go; she wasn't a professed sister yet. No lengthy process, no dispensation. Nothing too dreary or too public; Estelle could simply start another life.

Estelle couldn't exit secretly, though. The girl-group at Grace was tight-knit; they'd had their share of squabbles, but the loss of a fellow sister would feel like a limb was lopped off. Estelle felt obligated to say goodbye to these women, her women, so she did. When she told them about the signed forms, the date she would go, their eyes got wide and weary, they chattered among themselves, then to her. At least outwardly, Estelle seemed Lord-loving, efficient, pleasant. Some girls judged her decision, others asked her if they should go too, others thought she should have spent more time in discernment. They asked if she had fallen for someone in the city, if her family was all right, if she'd lost the faith. Estelle didn't know the truth herself, why she was leaving. She only knew the Soft Space in her heart, the space that had led her to Sisters of Grace in the first place, was telling her to go. The choice felt firmly right and supremely horrifying. So she was done; she told the women it was Her Time.

Now, Estelle had one last goodbye. Her mentor and faux mother, the reason she'd come to this place. The novitiate mistress, Sister Adriana. Estelle had to finish her exit interview in Adriana's office. Estelle hoped the process would be quick, but it wasn't. Estelle was soaked in sweat; the backs of her legs stuck to the chair. The South Florida air grew fat in the small room, and Adriana's air conditioner only slightly tempered the blast. Red flies swung through cracks in the window, stuck to Estelle's neck, bit hard, flitted off. Estelle's hair had grown loose, large, and curly, expanding beyond her shoulders. Sister Adriana, on the other hand, was composed; the heat didn't touch her. The older brunette wore a simple blue blazer and golden crucifix, her face pale and dry as baby powder. She twirled a pencil calmly. She readjusted her glasses, looked down at Estelle's papers then back to the young woman's face.

"You've turned in your keys," she said flatly. "You have a ride."

"Yes, ma'am." Estelle couldn't read Adriana's expression. "Mavis?"

"Yes," Estelle said, wiping her forehead. Adriana's eyes flashed. She licked her lips, positioned the eraser of the pencil at the tip of her chin. "All right."

Mavis was Estelle's real sister. She was famous around Grace for her huge entrances, irreverent language, and sharp remarks.

"You know, we'd never abandon you," Adriana said, sitting forward. "Remember that. You'll always have a soft place to fall if you feel alone. I was sorry to hear you'd leave before we went to the women's shelter in Kendall. If you stayed, those women would be blessed by you."

Estelle tried to block out rising guilt. She felt as if she were in some kind of reverse Garden of Eden; Sister Adriana was the serpent. She cared about Adriana, as a person. She cared about their service projects, and she'd appreciated her time at the family enrichment centers, homeless shelters, and nursing care facilities. She was also close to Adriana. Even though Adriana was Estelle's superior, they'd gotten along well. On purple nights the two would walk together in the convent gardens, after night prayers. They'd repeat memorized Psalms to each other, dream up fresh plans for advocacy programs. Adriana had once called Estelle a "true friend." Now, Adriana was in her official role. She was in charge of

Estelle's progress, and from Adriana's perspective, the older woman had failed her novice.

"I'm sorry," Adriana said. She pinched her temples. "We should keep going."

Estelle nodded.

Adriana's eyes swept Estelle, and Estelle looked right back at her. The Soft Space in Estelle's heart kept her strong, said, Do not waver, girl. She could hear it clearly this time. She'd accomplished what she needed to finish. Do not waver, girl.

"You know many women wrestle with the call to marriage. You might think it's your calling, but perhaps you are simply—"

"Nothing like that. Nothing to do with the call to marriage."

Estelle clicked her tongue. She'd repeated this phrase so many times. It seemed even Sister Adriana didn't believe Estelle. She thought Estelle was leaving for some romantic business. Estelle was disappointed but not surprised. Estelle's choices, that she made for herself, had nothing to do with an anonymous love. The sister let silence speak for her, and she shuffled through papers she'd probably already read.

"Okay. That's it then. I won't ask any more questions," the sister said. Adriana reached forward and gripped Estelle's hands. Estelle gripped her tiny hands back, loosely. Adriana let her go, fast. She balanced her small glasses at the end of her nose, slapped the paperwork, entered some numbers into her desktop computer. She didn't say anything else. She got up and led Estelle out of her office, down the polished walnut floors, and beside the straight-backed fiddle-leaf figs. There used to be a picture of the Blessed Maria on the white hallway walls, but it had since been removed.

Outside, on the porch, the grasses slumped with Miami's boulder-heavy heat. The slate clouds were belly-full, and the wet in the air made the firecracker flowers reek. Thin scrub jays cried. On the porch wing, Father Franco, Estelle's other mentor, was rocking back and forth in yellow gym clothes. He sat in a C shape on the swing, perching his phone on his paunch. His glasses, huge and gold-rimmed, slid to the bottom of his nose as he watched YouTube videos on his phone. When Estelle and Adriana passed him, he creakily got up.

"Well, she's outta here." He rose and threw his hands on the women's shoulders. "'How do you solve a problem like Estelle?' The disgrace!" Adriana politely removed her shoulder, as did Estelle. Estelle knew he was joking, but there was a bit of red underneath his words she didn't like. Father Franco smiled big to let her know he was kidding; his face was coral-colored, relaxed. Estelle liked him well enough. When she first met Franco, he hadn't seemed much like a priest to her, or at least not like the ones she'd known in New Orleans. He liked jokes, was somewhat charismatic, a little bit nerdy, and an obsessive *Battlestar Galactica* fan. Mavis said Franco would buy forty dollars' worth of weed from her whenever she came around. Estelle saw Franco smoking in the monastery garden sometimes while reading Saga comics. Nobody bothered him in these moments; he was smiling to himself and looked supremely pleased.

Adriana gave Estelle a long, tight hug. Estelle returned it weakly. The sister smelled like sawdust and Vaseline and Estelle swallowed bile. Adriana released her, roughly, left the two on the porch, and went back in the house. She slammed the door, a wreath of tulips rattling. Estelle wished Adriana had said something kind, or anything.

"Shit. Whoops," Father Franco whistled at Adriana's reaction. He placed a hand on Estelle's head. "Don't feel too bad, kid. She just internalizes everything. Thinks she's a failure and you're going to destroy yourself once you get out. As one does."

Estelle felt a little prick in the back of her head. The Soft Space in her heart was telling her to strengthen her insides, not to take Franco too seriously. She wasn't going to destroy herself after she left Grace. She was going to keep living just fine.

"And the thing is: you're still . . . innocent? I hate saying that because you're a grown woman. Not innocent-innocent. Should I use the word *vipers*? Watch out for vipers." Estelle started to block him out, but he went on. "Resist the occasion of temptation. That's what I'm supposed to tell you with performative acerbity. But seriously. You're going to need to—"

The pinching got harder. "Thank you, Father."

Franco shifted from one leg to the other and scratched the back of his neck. "Here's a story. Before I found the Lord, I was tripping balls. A lot. On one of those occasions, I was fireside with my friends in Sedona. I'm not supposed to tell you this, but since you're going to leave anyway, whatever. Back then, I thought I saw the face of Christ. See, my friend

Speck had bought this Halloween mask. It was Willem Dafoe as Jesus from *Last Temptation*, and it was so weirdly accurate, like custom-made. He had this mask on, and we were all there, staring at the fire. Then Speck-Jesus started rubbing his hands by the flame and he just, glowed. I was certain he was Christ. Speck-Jesus looked at me and started nodding. I thought Speck's nodding was Christ saying yes to me, and I didn't hear anything the Speck under that mask was actually saying. I just made up shit that made sense to my screwed-up head. I truly believed Speck-Jesus was telling me to go to this pool behind my friend's house. Speck-Jesus was like, 'The pool is God, go see God!' And let me tell you. The pool *wasn't* God, it wasn't even a pool, it was the interstate in front of Speck's place. I wandered out there, almost got hit by a semitruck, but I didn't, because one of my friends pulled me back. Look, I don't know the full point of this story, but some of the point is that some things look like God, but they're really just Speck in a Willem Dafoe mask agreeing with anything you want him to say. Sometimes, things look like a pool of God, but they're really a road full of speeding cars. Your job is to discern which is which. See . . ."

Estelle tried to pay attention. She generally got the point. Franco didn't know how many analogies Estelle had been given at this point, but they all amounted to "Don't let yourself get swallowed up by the Real World and by your sister Mavis." And as Franco was saying these things, Mavis's Volvo 960, the rust-lined blue junker, sputtered its way to the curb.

Franco turned around and followed Estelle's eyes. The car

screamed to a stop. Estelle watched her sister's shadow slap the wheel, bend down, and fish around in the car, probably for a lighter. Mavis found one, it seemed. She threw a cigarette in her mouth, rolled down the window. Mavis tugged the door, kicked it a few times open, and she fell out of the car. She unfolded her long body out of the Volvo and stood up. There was Mavis, in her regal, messy, dangerous glory. She was braless, as usual, her small breasts nearly bouncing out of her black shirt as she walked. There she was, in knee-high boots and acid-washed jeans that gripped her meaty thighs. Mavis shoved the door shut with a high-heeled foot and leaned against the car. She took a few puffs from her cigarette and blew smoke from her mouth over her shoulder. Seeing Estelle and Franco, she grinned, waved a big hand. Estelle raised her fingers and Father Franco winced. Mavis flicked the cigarette onto the sidewalk, stamped it dead, and strode toward Estelle and Franco. She approached the two with her typical panther-smooth walk. She slapped her hands together.

"Franco! My *love*," she said happily to the priest. Franco blushed and looked back at the rectory building. Mavis said, "Down to blaze? Parting party before I bring my girl back? What you want?" Franco rolled his eyes nervously and checked around the premises. "I'm okay today," he said, but he kept his gaze long on Mavis, like he was considering it. Mavis balanced a new cigarette in her mouth; her gaze swept Franco and Estelle. She nodded with her chin at the squinting priest. "No? Cool. Your loss." She threw her eyes at Estelle, took in another draw, exhaled. Mavis flapped her hand at Estelle. "Leggo, my dear." Estelle followed her sister to the Volvo, without looking back at Father Franco. Franco helped Estelle roll her suitcase to the car, and Mavis stuck the cigarette in the corner of her mouth. She snatched Estelle's bag from Franco, threw it over her shoulder, chucked it in the back seat. The priest drifted away from them, and Estelle could hear him mumbling prayers for her. Estelle didn't want to hear them.

Estelle fell onto the passenger seat and moved aside burger wrappers and coffee-wet trash. Estelle could see a slit in Adriana's office window; she was watching them. Estelle imagined at least some of her cohort were snatching glimpses at her too or they were singing goodbye. Franco yelled something like, "Take care of yourself!" and Mavis gave him a peace sign.

Estelle stared at the House of Grace building. It was two-floored, orange-bricked, and flanked by a garden full of red-leafed hibiscuses and porterweeds.

While Mavis clicked back to the car and got in, Estelle kept looking. Estelle mouthed, "So long," and knew nobody could see her lips moving.

In the car, everything felt like a different kind of normal. Estelle had been in the convent for nearly three years, but she'd spent most of her life with Mavis, in New Orleans, where they'd both grown up and gone to school. Her father, a theater director, and mother, an actress, had passed when they were children. Most of Estelle's life had been watching Mavis playing saxophone with their uncle, a jazzman who, like their parents, had enjoyed a considerable following in his youth. After Estelle was assaulted one night in New Orleans, she dropped out of college to regroup, and Mavis finished her degree in music history and started teaching locally. Mavis was given a teaching job at a small nonprofit in Miami, and she brought Estelle with her. In South Florida, Mavis taught piano through a few college programs and played gigs in Fort Lauderdale and West Palm. Estelle got close to Adriana then, who, looking to develop relationships with local nonprofits, had attended one of Mavis's music workshops. Adriana saw Estelle and felt for her. Estelle had enrolled at MDC to finish her last credits and was still recovering from the shadowman who had thrown her against the wall on Bourbon Street and shoved his fingers inside of her. The life Adriana offered Estelle was quiet, altruistic, women-centered, and flower-rimmed. Estelle loved the idea of Sisters of Grace as a place of peace, safety, and spirituality. No press and push of the nasty world. Estelle started to frequent Sisters of Grace on her own; she'd stride through their fresh-bloomed garden with Adriana and talk about God and moving past darkness and life challenges. She'd spend nights communing with the grasses outside of Mavis's apartment, speaking love to the sky. Estelle was convinced that the convent was her calling. Mavis wasn't a fan of Estelle's decision, as she thought the church was patriarchal bullshit that ultimately repressed women regardless of the rhetoric, but Estelle tried to convince her otherwise. She told Mavis Sisters of Grace had numerous social justice programs, they did quality service work, and that she didn't have to be a virgin to take a vow of chastity. Mavis didn't budge on her views, but she loved her sister, so she supported her. Mavis supported her even when she received a better job as a director of a children's music center in Fort Pierce. She moved two hours away from Miami and still came back weekly to visit Estelle at the House of Grace.

Now Estelle's vision had changed. While Mavis outwardly seemed restless and spike-filled, she was actually sharp-minded and focused on her music career. Mavis had consistently worked teaching gigs, consistently had money and an apartment and supported herself, and while not religious in any way, she followed her own voice deeply. Estelle, meanwhile, always felt drenched in spirits and swamps of voices, enough so that she could end up anywhere, or nowhere. Estelle only had the Soft Space in her heart to guide her. Was she going the right way now?

Regardless, Estelle was where she'd always been, even as a teenager. In the passenger seat of Mavis's car, sitting on her fast-food wrappers and plastic bags full of tissues. Inhaling the thick scent of cigarette smoke and kush, watching Mavis's high-necked profile framed against the slow-moving traffic.

"Man, I wanted to hotbox with Franco," Mavis said. "He wasn't going to do it in front of Mama A. We should have taken him with us, I'd show him some nerdy shit. Where's my gum? Fuck."

Estelle pressed her face against the glass. The more the car banged and lurched on I-95 N, the more Estelle remembered she was speeding toward a rootless life. Estelle felt free, happy, insane. The Soft Space in her heart said nothing.

"Sorry," Mavis said gently. "Anyway." She leaned her wrist on the wheel. "A$AP Rocky. He's got this song called 'Praise the Lord.' For your Liberation Day."

"That's a good song." Estelle watched an egret balance itself on the highway railing. Her tongue was dry, tasted like cotton.

Mavis drove through the turnpike's Easy Pass. "Gregorian shit goes well over an 808. That's some shit I might do when I've got downtime."

Mavis put on the song. A$AP blasted hoarsely through the damaged speakers. Estelle tried to hear what the Soft Space was saying, but it thrummed in her body, not offering much.

They hit another patch of traffic. Mavis lit a cigarette and smoked it out of her window. Some guy was honking his horn at them, and Mavis threw him a middle finger. He honked louder. He started cussing in Spanish and Mavis pumped her fist to A$AP's beat. The man pulled in front of her and she sat on the horn. "Hey," she said to Estelle, midway through the face-off, "I'm proud of you."

Mavis let up on the brake, swerved in front of the guy, played some stop-and-start games with him that made Estelle's stomach revolt. She lurched forward, gripped the door. Mavis looked over at her sister, laid up apologetically, and swerved into the middle lane. The guy passed them, rolling down his window to screech at her again. Mavis turned up A$AP and sang along. She winked at the man, and he moved on. Mavis threw the cigarette out the window. Estelle's face started cracking. She pressed her forehead on the window, so Mavis couldn't see her. She wanted to cry.

Estelle could feel Mavis looking over at her, but she couldn't look back. "My love," Mavis said. "The world is going to be shitty whether you've got a habit on or not. So you might as well 'Praise the Lord,' as A$AP says. That's the most religious thing you're going to get out of me."

"I know. I get it," Estelle said.

"If you wanted to stay in Grace, that would be okay too. If you want to talk to the sky and ocean by yourself, you can. I wish I could hear Some Voice talk, but the world is always streaking around me. Like I'm in some kaleidoscope and everything looks bright, but it's all the same. But I support whatever the fuck you want. And the thing is, you did good, you didn't fail at anything. In fact you learned how to get an edge, you learned . . ."

"I'm fine," Estelle cut her sister off. She wasn't in the mood.

Estelle couldn't see anything anymore. She couldn't hear the church bells. She couldn't smell flowers. She was leaving her little home in Miami because of a hunch that clenched hard in her belly. The blue-pink skies burned above her. A new egret landed on another railing. It squawked and she couldn't hear the sound humming through its beak.

Adjacent to the House of Grace's chapel door, there was a massive image of the Maria. She was white as a spotlight, her arms raised to the sky as huge beams of ivory tumbled from her hands to her prim feet. Pink-skinned babies clustered at her feet, their gazes fixed upon Maria's beauty with unremitting adoration. The two Black girls in the convent, Bianca and Estelle, would look at this Maria and think about her bright face. They'd grown used to the other idols in the house, but this Maria's face was bleached and cold. She didn't feel like home.

Bianca was Estelle's friend, and she was always talking about leaving the convent but never did. The other girls called her Troublemaker because she openly fought with her directress during her postulant process, defied teachers during patristics and canon law classes, and turned down most friendships. Estelle couldn't remember much of what Bianca had done to piss everyone off. She was always in some room receiving a loud voice from someone. One night, Bianca finally did her Biggest Thing. On that late blue night, Estelle heard a knock on her door. She got up quickly and answered her friend.

Bianca pulled the knob toward her, so Estelle could only see her through a crack. "You like art, right? I saw you were good at it. I saw you drawing outside."

"I'm okay."

"I'm going to leave. But first, I want to paint that Mary's face black. You know the one. But I'm not great at art and I want it to look nice."

Estelle considered the things she was saying. "Yeah?"

"You'll come? I'm a little scared."

Part of Estelle wanted to join in. That part didn't care about her relationship with Adriana or the girls or the original painter. She looked at Bianca and wondered why she'd decided to kamikaze herself so definitively.

Estelle started to say no, but sounding like Mavis, she said: "Hell yeah."

Bianca came back with supplies, the good ones, she'd stolen from the art room. They snuck out to the hallway, where the painting hung. Estelle told Bianca they'd have to do it quickly. Bianca said fine. She took the nape of the neck, colored it black all the way to the shoulders. Estelle worked on shading the face and revealed arms. They did their best to make the black color regal, beautiful. Estelle didn't have any sort of reservations during this business. She should have, she thought she would, but she didn't. God hadn't painted that picture. Nobody knew who painted the picture; it was a donation from a past church, so she wasn't hurting the artist. When they were finished, the new Black Maria's eyes gazed back at them. They both wrote on her lavender dress, in golden cursive scrawl, "Holy." Estelle stared at the finished image. It wasn't the disaster she thought it would be. This Maria seemed more like home now; she looked comfortable and kind.

Estelle thought about her dead mother, this woman she barely knew. If Estelle added some eyelashes and mascara, she would look like the poster of Estelle's mother, the one she kept folded under her pillow.

That night, Estelle thought someone would catch them,

but nobody did. It took a full day for Adriana to find Estelle in her room, even though the picture was hung in an obvious location and the gossip had begun immediately.

The next afternoon, Estelle was preparing to go to the gardens, and Adriana stopped her, called her into her office. Adriana was frowning hard and wiping her face. "Bianca is going to be expelled. Because she defaced the Maria. I know she's your friend, so I wanted to tell you that."

Estelle waited for her implication in the crime, but it didn't happen. Adriana's eyes swept Estelle. "I hope you're all right, if that happens. Know that I'll always be there for you."

Estelle realized Bianca had taken the blame alone, which wasn't fair. Adriana was simply trying to make sure Estelle stayed.

Estelle shrugged. "The Maria's not defaced."

Adriana let out a sigh and rubbed her temples. "Look. This isn't time for politics. That was our property."

"You could call it a historical art project. It's not worth her being expelled," Estelle pressed.

"It is. It was the last straw," Adriana fought back, then lowered her voice. "She doesn't want to be here. That's clear. I just want you to know that we care about you."

"I helped her," Estelle finally said. "I colored the face and neck. I like the Maria now."

Adriana opened her mouth, closed it. She turned toward the window then spun back to Estelle. "She cajoled you because you're an artist. I suspected as much—"

"I helped her willingly."

"I know you, Estelle," Adriana insisted, getting closer and louder. "You remind me of myself. You came to us confused and hurt. The world gobbled you up. You have shown observable growth in your faith in God and you're an integral part of our charism. As such, you need to be here. Bianca's already lost."

Estelle shook her head. She wasn't like anyone. She never liked when people said she was "just like them," when they barely knew her. Adriana let Estelle off, said she was merely following her friend. Bianca would receive a lesser punishment, but she could stay. Estelle went to find Bianca to tell her the news, but she couldn't. Bianca left the house voluntarily that night, without saying goodbye.

Mavis lived in a two-story town house on Hutchinson Island, two blocks away from the public beaches, with a roommate she rarely saw. The place was lime-painted and small; clematis flowers twisted and wound their way around Mavis's white fence. As Mavis dragged Estelle's bags down the thin sidewalk, Estelle felt a rush of familiarity again. Weed smells and sage snaked through the front door. Mavis inserted her key into the lock, kicked the jamb a few times, and they were back inside.

Mavis and Estelle stood in the place for a few minutes. Estelle was short, at Mavis's elbow. Mavis hovered above her, in her grand height. Mavis threw an arm around her sister and leaned down to kiss her head. Estelle rested against her, inhaling sandalwood and cigarette smoke. Estelle's body exhaled, finally.

"Look, kid," Mavis said. "I know this isn't as nice as Grace, but it's your spot." The living room was Mavis-clean, which meant the black leather couch didn't have socks wedged in its crevices, but it still had a film of sand from the beach. The rugs were hastily vacuumed and towels were tucked in corners. Bins of miscellaneous junk were stacked atop each other and stacks of dog-eared novels were stuffed beside the patio door. Nothing was clean, per se, but it was clear Mavis had made a huge effort. Mavis grabbed Estelle's hand and dragged her to an empty room.

Mavis had set up a small bed in the corner. The sheets smelled like hydrangeas and the old wood of the walls. Atop a wicker desk sat a picture of Mavis and Estelle grinning on South Beach, a magazine photo of their mother Mavis had framed, and an African Maria prayer card. A bouquet of red orchids, Estelle's mother's favorite, according to her diaries, sat in the middle of the desk.

Estelle stood at the doorway. She bit her lips. She wanted to cry, but she couldn't yet, because if she started she'd just blubber away. She wanted to stay still today.

"Thanks," she choked.

"Oh, the desk. I hate all this shit, but I thought you might like it. Made it look like your old place, but new. I don't know," Mavis explained. She wheeled Estelle's bags into the room and jumped onto her bed. She took out her phone and looked at it for a second, put it back in her pocket. "So, here's the deal. I promised this cat I was gonna catch his gig tonight. He's got this preshow thing downtown. I was gonna go, but today's your Liberation Day, so I'm gonna text him nah."

"Go," Estelle said.

Mavis started to say something, then took it back, tried again. "You can come with me? At least to the party, which should be tame. This isn't Miami, so you don't have to worry about people acting up too much. Don't know if this is zero to one hundred real quick, though."

White sun shone through the window slats. Estelle walked over and pulled up the pane, sniffed the air. No ocean scents yet, but she could feel the waves nearby.

"The distraction might be good," she said. "I'll go." She hadn't been to a party, or around new people, in a long time. She didn't know about going out into the world now, but she also didn't want to be alone.

Mavis cocked an eyebrow. "I'll watch out for you. I'm a damn wreck, but I'll take care of you."

"I know," Estelle said.

Estelle spent many of her nights talking to the Soft Space in her heart. The space spoke and her thoughts followed in suit and there she was, wrapped warmly in contemplation.

She'd think about her mother, first. Estelle's mother, that Black Boricua actress, was born and raised on the island. Her name was Alejandra. Alejandra moved to Hartford, Connecticut, in her midteens. She was popular in island commercials, and when she came to the States some Puerto Ricans already knew her shining face. She'd met Rodrigo, Estelle and Mavis's father, in a coffee shop while she was working as a barista in New Haven. He told her she was special, called her his muse. Shivering and young, according to her mother's diary, Estelle and Mavis's mother loved and married fast. Alejandra appeared in Rodrigo's earliest plays, and a few of his works made it off Broadway. Things had gone well enough, except their father was a serial cheater and a consummate suffering artist, and he struggled with severe depression. He eventually killed himself one night, right after a New Year's Eve party. Shortly after, their mother was diagnosed with melanoma and discovered she was pregnant with Mavis and Estelle. Their mother died three years after Mavis and Estelle were born.

Mavis wanted nothing to do with their parents. She thought they were lame and pointless; she was short like that. When Estelle brought the two up, Mavis would call them "dead fuckers who couldn't live for their own fucking kids." She'd take a drag out of her cigarette and move on to the next topic. Mavis lived, violently, in the moment. She hated the past and only somewhat looked ahead to the future. If her parents weren't around, she didn't care about them. Or at least that's what Mavis said. Mavis cared deeply about things but would never admit it. On the other hand, Estelle treasured the images of her mother and read her diary often. She'd found all the pictures of Alejandra when she was at the height of her popularity. Sometimes her mother wore long wigs, sometimes she had coiffed curls. There was a picture of her,

Estelle's favorite, where her mother's arms were stretched out, her pink, sparkling mouth wide. Purple streaks were painted across her face, and, in bold scrawl, the paper had written, "La Estrella." The Star. Her hair was huge and Afroed, in imitation of Celia Cruz, and her skin was layered with glittering violet. A star.

Estelle wondered what her mother would think of her, while she was alone, in her room at the convent. La Estrella.

The Soft Space in Estelle's heart was always there when she drifted to sleep. One night at the House of Grace, Estelle fell asleep, then awoke feeling new. Estelle was sweating; her face felt bee-stung. She tried to sleep again, and the closer she got to real slumber, the more she could feel her face and body shifting. She was mutating into a different woman. That night she dreamed hard. About the Maria they'd browned. About the person she'd been before that boy in New Orleans took her. About Adriana and Mavis. The more she thought about those faces, the more it felt right to go. She didn't know exactly why yet, but these women were leading her someplace. The Soft Space held her close and she fell asleep.

At Mavis's preparty, even at five o'clock in the afternoon, there were moving bodies. There were moving bodies stuffed in vermilion corners, on the glossy black floor, clustered around poppy-red tables; they were nose-lengths away from gold-painted statues of flexing naked men. A DJ was playing Afrobeat, a band was setting up nearby. The moving bodies that weren't talking or pinching wineglasses or throwing back beer were packed tight together. Some were wriggling, others shuddering hips, some were talking into the necks of other bodies. Estelle could smell new wine, Eau Fraiche cologne, and chalk. She hadn't been around this kind of environment—brim-packed and life-full—in so long she forgot it could exist. Mavis took Estelle's hand, led her to the back corner of the gallery. She plopped down on a red velvet couch and crossed her legs. Mavis stretched out her arm on the sofa and fingered the bangles on her wrists, a nervous habit she'd picked up to give herself space between cigarettes. Near instantly, a group of people Estelle didn't know leapt over to Mavis. Two of them, a tall white man in a bucket hat and a Black woman with tortoiseshell glasses, were shooting question after question at Mavis. Mavis gestured for Estelle to sit down next to her, and she did. The people were Mavis's work friends, musicians too. Mavis engaged them in light chatter while mentioning Estelle every so often so her sister could feel included. One of the girls told Estelle she liked her dress. Estelle panicked, for a moment thinking she was wearing her formless dark shift, designed for the days Grace girls went out into the world. When Estelle looked down, she remembered herself again. Mavis had given her a taupe kaftan that only slightly showed her curves and ankle-high leather boots. Estelle was trendy but comfortable. While Mavis and the group talked, Estelle's gaze flitted back to the bodies.

They were dazzling. All of them, every one. The long and short, wide and petite, the toe-walkers and flat-footed, the luminous-skinned and smooth-faced. The hems of cocoa, Black, and white bodies swishing and floating by; they were glorious. The Spanish tongues prattling, the light hair streaked with pink, the nose-ringed, the ringleted curls sizzling and explosive, the straight hair swinging thickly, the wigs front-laced and fine; they were all stunning. These moving bodies twisted and shook and rose. The music thumped louder, and the dancing bodies swung and dipped. The bodies raised hands and clapped, waved at the ceiling lights.

Now that she saw these bodies, alive, she thought they were just as beautiful as her mother. She switched her eyes back at Mavis. Mavis was alone now, her legs spread open defiantly; her stilettos sharply dug into the floor. She was smoking brazenly, near-bored, her black fedora low on her eyes. Smoke dribbled from the corners of her lips and she took another drag of her cigarette. New people approached her but nobody got close when they saw Mavis's eyes. Estelle knew Mavis. She wasn't unhappy; she was taking a break from being around people. Even at parties, Mavis needed moments alone.

Estelle though, she looked around the room. She was perched next to Mavis, like a handmaiden to a queen. Estelle's hair was pulled tight in a bun and she shook it down. She leaned over to her sister, kissed her on the cheek, and Mavis blinked herself out of her trance. Estelle motioned toward the crowd and Mavis rubbed Estelle's shoulder and told her to "go on, cuídate." Estelle glided into the groups of bodies, and most people opened space for her. She stayed at a safe distance; she wanted to be around them but not touched, not yet. She wasn't tied to any of these bodies; she was merely one of them. Somebody reached for her skin, and she touched theirs back, kindly, curiously. A girl got in her ear and whispered something sweet-sounding, and Estelle shivered. A man swung around and said she was beautiful then moved on respectfully. The Afrobeat switched to salsa, then back to Afrobeat, and Estelle wound her hips; she found the right rhythm each new time, her feet knew the best steps even if they weren't exactly correct. She felt holiness throb from the shaking bodies, from her own body looking for ways to fit into sounds she'd always known and had just discovered. Warmth throbbed in her waist and chest. She felt high and sacred. The Soft Space in her heart told her all was well and it was good to dance.

When Estelle got tired, she separated from the energy she'd absorbed and let the heat cool. She found Mavis in the same corner, on the same plush couch. When Estelle appeared, Mavis stood up, wrapped her arms around her. "I got a little worried, but you were good . . . ," Mavis whispered to her sister. Mavis swallowed, fell back onto the couch, and the musicians around her petted Estelle. Estelle joined her sister again. She felt wildly at ease and would be fine sitting there next to her warm sister all night, not saying a thing. Just watching the bodies and joining them whenever she pleased. Not needing protection, Estelle could leave and dance whenever she desired. Her sister and the Soft Space in her heart were close and obliging. Estelle let herself sink into the couch and the music stretched out, rolled louder and louder. It washed her, washed her.

At some point, several dances later, Mavis asked Estelle about the secret person.

"The night is gonna go long," Mavis explained. "This guy I'm waiting for hasn't shown up yet, and he's probably going to go on way late. But I wanted to get home early tonight. For you. Sorry for your Liberation Day."

"I'm happy," Estelle said.

Mavis sucked her teeth. "How liberated do you feel?"

"I feel okay."

Mavis stared at Estelle long, her arm still stretched over her sister on the couch. She scratched Estelle's shoulder.

"You didn't leave Grace for any kind of love business. You always say that."

Estelle near sighed. If it weren't Mavis asking, she would have cut this conversation short. "That's true."

"And that's why, if there was someone you liked, you couldn't even like 'em properly. That's what sucks."

"Come on," Estelle said.

"Did you ever have a thing for Bianca? I always wondered. She was cute. But maybe that's just me projecting because she was my type."

Estelle rolled her eyes. Bianca was pretty, funny, and gone. Bianca was important to her. That much was clear, but Estelle didn't understand their connection fully.

"Someone else then?"

Estelle didn't say anything. She didn't want to talk about romantic things. Love for another woman or man wasn't the reason she left.

"Give me your phone," Mavis said. Estelle shook her head. "Nope."

"Come on," Mavis laughed, "I promise I won't do anything weird."

"I don't believe you."

"Good instincts. Look, I have an idea."

Estelle reluctantly handed over her phone to Mavis, and Mavis proceeded to scroll through her messages. Estelle tried to get her cell back, but Mavis held her away.

"All right. That's the one. This guy?"

She held the phone up. A series of text bubbles flashed at Estelle. She saw her last conversation with Mateo Vasquez, a student in her class at the MDC. He was born and raised in New Orleans, roughly her height, with gray eyes and lisle-smooth skin. He'd been a drifter too and had lived in several cities before he settled on Miami. He always defended Estelle's personhood against their class's resident asshole. The other boys in Estelle's class knew she was studying to be a nun, and they put on airs to protect her supposed (and nonexistent) virginity. Like many other sisters, Estelle had lost her virginity when she was in high school to a guy she sort of liked. These boys in her class, however, just secretly dreamed of fucking a virgin nun. But Mateo was different; he was a kindred spirit, and she was admittedly attracted to him. He treated her with respect that had nothing to do with her being a nun. Regardless, throughout her class, she didn't feel safe around men who weren't Father Franco, or, in doses, Mateo.

Mavis scrolled through more messages and Estelle tried to stop her, but Mavis had already caught the story.

"Your long-ass text bubbles and his instant replies. I'm right?"

Estelle tugged at her hair over and over. Mavis's eyes roamed the screen.

"Wow. Yeah, this one's kind of sweet. Hmm. Change of plans. I'm calling him."

Estelle made a grab for the phone and Mavis dodged her easily. In seconds, Mavis was on the phone. Estelle's pulse picked up as she heard it ring. Mateo swiftly answered. She buckled over her knees, terrified and embarrassed and thrilled.

"Yo," Mavis said. "Ey? Nah. This is Estelle's sister. Guess what? She's not a nun no more. No, we're in Fort Pierce. Now that she's in the free world, will you take her out sometime? I'll bring her back to Miami, I promise."

Estelle started shivering more.

"Seriously? That's perfect," Mavis said. She tossed the phone to Estelle, and she clumsily caught it.

"He's driving up tonight."

"No. It's too far." Estelle couldn't believe Mateo would be willing to drive two hours up to see her.

"Not too far for this guy. He volunteered, says he's got nothing to do and wants to see you." Mavis stretched back on the couch. "Good. I want *you* to see something."

———

Before the opening act, the moving bodies settled into corners and sighed in sync. They stopped their superficial networking and sought skin-safety and kinship. Around this time, Mateo slipped in through the front door. Estelle felt him come in immediately. His dark curls were oiled back. He moved nervously; he was searching the chattering faces, the red-black lights eddied in his eyes. He wore a leather coat over a yellow plaid shirt; he was slightly dressed up.

Estelle wiped the sweat from her hands on her dress. She thought about calling him over, but she couldn't work her lips right. Mavis was midconversation with one of the drummers from the band. She noticed Estelle's jitters and threw a hand over her sister's shoulder. Mavis waved vigorously.

"I don't know who I'm looking for, but I know where you're looking," she laughed. Mateo saw the two then. He flashed his fence post teeth and his dimples deepened. He ducked under a few willowy men and made his way over to them.

Mateo stood barely an inch taller than Estelle, but she felt as if he were looming over her. She opened her mouth, and he opened his mouth, and neither of them said a thing. Mavis excused herself from her friend and shook Mateo's hand. Just as Mateo was saying, "Hey there, Estelle," Mavis said:

"Hey, man, thanks so much for coming. You can stay at this party, but all they have are those tiny-ass cheeses and stuffed mushrooms, no real food. Y'all can go somewhere else, if you want."

"Sure, of course," Mateo said. He smiled at Estelle. She relaxed a little. He was just her friend from English Composition II. That was all. He plucked a finger at the door and said, "You want to go for a walk, get some food? I assume you've been here all night."

"I have," she said. "But it's been wonderful."

Mateo leaned in and Estelle bit her tongue. He said, "I've got to hear more about that."

"And so you shall," Mavis said. "Be good, kids. And be fucking right to her." Mavis half-smiled, her eyes sharp, and Mateo nodded quickly.

Mateo reached forward and touched Estelle's upper back respectfully to lead her through the crowd. His warm hand pricked her nerves, made her heart bang around. She was used to merely liking him, to pushing down any kind of attraction. Now that she was given permission to feel anything she liked, she felt blushy and new. A dance track started; the kick and snare drums roared, leapt up through the floor and tickled their shoes. As the bass grew, their shoes shuffled along and their hips swayed, electrically close.

Mateo opened the door for Estelle. They both stood under the flickering lights of the gallery roof. A dragonfly flapped over Mateo's head and he ignored it. He suggested a nearby pizza spot he'd found on Yelp, and Estelle agreed. They passed beige condo buildings and rows of palm trees puncturing the sidewalks. They took a left on Melody Lane and walked down Orange Avenue in silence, stepping over hearts and happy faces scrawled in chalk on the sidewalks.

Eventually, Mateo said, "Did you have a reason, or did you just know it was right to go?"

The Soft Space in Estelle's heart sighed.

"I just felt it," she said. "I had reasons but didn't need them."

"Of course," Mateo said. He glanced up at the pinkening sky. "Back in New Orleans, I was almost a nurse, a baseball player, and a chef all in one year. Every time I started one of those things, I was so sure I was on the right path. But now I'm just an older student at FIU. I feel like I'm in this prolonged waiting period. Just waiting to figure out where I'm going, where I should move, all that. I want to try something else, but I don't. It's weird."

"Right. I get it," Estelle said. She was happy Mateo was opening up to her. She didn't mind if he was trying to relate to her wholly dissimilar life. They crossed the street and moved past a row of gray-painted eateries.

"Sh–crap," Mateo said. Estelle thought it was funny he was trying not to cuss in front of her. He went on, "I'm not saying my life and yours are the same. I'm really not. You're going through something huge. I just would see you all the time. Studying so hard in our class with those assholes—jerks, I mean—all around you. Studying so hard while you had this other calling. I respected that. You were just the most committed person I'd ever seen."

Estelle bit her teeth. She was never committed to anything really. She simply allowed herself to go along with various paths and was too stubborn to give up. And now here she was, fully wayward, without any clear direction. "I'm not a committed person. I left the thing I was most committed to. I thought leaving Grace was the right thing to do, but that's not what committed people do. I didn't tough it out."

"Ugh! I'm saying this all wrong." Mateo rubbed his temples. "You're doing the right thing if it's the right thing for you. Honestly, I'm just nervous. I was really excited to see you and then your sister tells me all of this new information and it messed with my head."

"You're fine!" she laughed. "I'm messing with your head?" She wiggled her eyebrows.

"Yes!" Mateo poked her. "You're messing with my head, just being yourself. And you're great. That's what's messing with me."

"Me being myself or me no longer being in the convent?"

"Both. And not in a bad way. I don't know how to phrase this and maybe I shouldn't say it. Bah." He looked up. Lorenzo's Pizza, with its steel letters and ash-colored walls, stood in front of them. Mateo dropped the subject and switched to lighter things. Over pizza, they slipped back into friendly banter. Estelle realized she hadn't spent much time talking to Mateo; she only saw him in class. They texted every so often about New Orleans or shared memes, and she always asked him about schoolwork, but she hadn't gone out with him one-on-one. And now here he was, in her new city, on his own accord. They laughed about different ways to fold the pizza. Mateo went on about how much he loved his parents, how his brother had run away at ten and had recently come back into his life. Estelle told him about Father Franco and Adriana, about Bianca and the room Mavis had set up for her. She described the Soft Space in her heart, and all of these things Mateo listened to seriously. He leaned forward, his eyes wide with interest. After they finished the pizza, Mateo helped Estelle out of her chair, and they exited. There was plenty of time left in the night and Mateo offered to walk Estelle to a mural he'd caught near his car on Orange. As they ventured up the street, Estelle felt giddy. Her belly was warm with food, her pulse was shivery. Mateo was lovely company. She liked the rush of being inches apart from him. Every so often, he'd ask permission to move her away from an oncoming drunk or couple, and when he touched her, she felt a surge of electricity and a strange kind of happiness.

The mural was on the side of an abandoned white building near a set of rust-covered railroad tracks. It was of a Black woman, enormous and glorious. She was strong-eyed and donned a felt hat. Daisies were wedged in her short curls, and a rose sat snugly behind her ear. Bursts of orange, green, and lavender surged from her eyelashes. She held a small notebook and stood in front of a long stretch of ocean. Mateo edged in a little closer to her.

"She reminded me of you, this woman. Just the eyes. Or the presence."

"That's Zora Neale Hurston," Estelle said. "She came here, to Fort Pierce, in her last years to start again."

Estelle smiled. The image was of Zora, but it was drawn

ambiguously enough that it could be any Black woman, freeing herself from something. It could be Estelle, Mavis, her mother, the Black Maria. Looking holy.

Mateo swallowed big. He looked off at the street, at the swaths of moving bodies on the road, clamoring or pressed close. He asked Estelle, gently, if he could move her out of people-traffic again, and she let him. This time, he stayed next to her and didn't back away. Estelle felt her attraction to him in searing colors.

"Hey," he started. He licked his lips, took a step back, changing his mind. He said something else: "I don't remember if I locked my car. I have that Miami-fear in me that someone's going to break in and take everything."

"Let's check," Estelle said. She was disappointed but didn't know why. She followed him back to his car, and he arrived at his sedan.

"I'm embarrassing," he mumbled and cursed to himself. He checked his locks, and they were fine. He relocked his doors, fumbled with his keys, and dropped them. Estelle picked the keys up for him, and he reached for them a little too quickly. He let his hand stay on hers, sweetly. He smiled his dimpled smile, then blinked rapidly and pocketed the keys. He leaned against the car and folded his arms. Estelle could see his biceps bulge from his jacket, and she wondered why she was looking so hard at them.

"Mierda," he said. "I know that you just got out, and I know I'm not supremely religious, but I'm like . . . I don't know. I've always felt . . . Do you know what I'm trying to say?" His gaze was kind and perfect. Estelle, in that moment, was terrified with joy.

She shook her head.

"I came up here to see you. And I thought it'd look weird because the drive was so long and I came on short notice. But I really, really wanted to see you. And Mavis told me That Thing. That you just got out. And I didn't want to impose. But I came anyway. And I came back to the car, but I don't want you to think that I'm up to something. I'm just worried you're going to think I'm one of Those Guys, but I'm not one of Those Guys. I just wanted to check my car. I don't want anything from you, Estelle. Shit, I suck at this."

Estelle didn't know what was happening, but her opinion hadn't changed. She still liked him. "Okay."

"But the problem is that I do feel like . . . ugh. Like I want to say it, but I don't want to be one of Those Guys."

Estelle's pulse picked up again. "It's okay. Say what you want to say."

"Are you sure?"

"Yes."

He moved closer to her and said, softly, "I want to kiss you. But I want to be respectful. You can say no."

"You can."

Mateo's eyebrows flew up. "Yeah?"

"Yeah."

He leaned forward and kissed her. His lips tasted heaven-like. He pulled back and stared at Estelle, then brushed the hair from her face.

They both stared at each other, happy and awkward. Then Estelle pulled him toward her, and he kissed her again.

She didn't know what she was doing, and neither did he. She didn't know why she was kissing him, and maybe she did. Her body burned hot and wild and guiltless. When his breath got rougher, she broke away.

"I have to stop," she said. "I want to keep going, but . . ."

"Oh God," Mateo said. He nearly fell back into his car. "I screwed up. And the virgin thing. I forgot. I came on too strong. I wasn't trying to—"

"No, I'm not talking about virginity," she said. She didn't feel like having the virginity talk with him. This was a man she enjoyed being around; he wasn't her past. "I like you. I always have."

"Me too," Mateo said, looking simultaneously relieved and ill at ease.

"I'm sorry if I'm being confusing." She let out a similar sigh of frustration.

"You're not. Maybe I'm being too forward."

"You're not. It's not about you."

They went silent again. Mateo's eyes dimmed, like he was trying to figure her out. "Would you go back? To the . . . nunnery. Whatever you call it? If things don't work out here, with the rest of us?"

Estelle said, "I made my decision."

Mateo nodded. He gnawed his lips, his dimple faint but apparent.

Estelle went on, "I'm sorry if I inconvenienced you

tonight. Mavis called you, and now I'm not sure what to do next. Where I'm going . . ." She trailed off. She knew everything she said sounded like lies, but it was all true.

"You don't have to go anywhere," he said carefully. "I get it. I really get it."

"I do like you." Estelle couldn't find the proper words. She wanted to keep kissing Mateo, she wanted to see him again, but the Soft Space in her heart was telling her she didn't have any kind of plan with this man. She shouldn't have a plan for anything, not yet. This morning she'd said goodbye to Father Franco and Adriana, and now, at the end of the day, she was kissing a boy from her class outside of a mural of another free woman who reminded her of her mother. It was too much, too soon to make any kind of decision.

Mateo reached out and held Estelle. She hugged him back, hard.

"Relax. You'll be fine." He reached forward, took her hand, squeezed it. She gripped his. He was reaching for her face as she was grabbing his jaw and their faces fell into each other. He wrapped his arms around her, and she was in his hair, and he pushed her against the car, and she kissed him back, and teeth were clashing, and nobody was acting soft anymore, and she felt his erection through his jeans, and she pushed against him because she liked that feeling. He felt wonderful pressed against her clothed body, and she wanted him. He leaned her against the hood of his car and kissed her again. She wondered what she was supposed to do. Was this moment supposed to change her mind about her future? She couldn't be with this good man, Mateo, even though she desperately wanted to. Why had Mavis called him?

Mateo broke from Estelle at the same time she'd decided to tear herself away.

"Okay," he said. His face was sweaty, eyes red. He jumped off of her and readjusted his pants. She felt flushed and confused and hungry for flesh. She hadn't felt any of that before and was suddenly angry at Mavis for putting both of them in that situation.

Mateo turned back to her. Their eyes roamed each other and nobody had anything good to say. She wasn't supposed to think about tomorrow. So she wouldn't. But she felt relieved. Relieved she could like Mateo, that her body and mind could open up to a man like him, even for a few hours.

He reached forward and brushed the dark hair out of her eyes once more. They were going to break now. He'd come all this way, but they were going to break. She couldn't tell if she was leaving him or if he was leaving her. He was handsome and fun; she'd seen girls look at him in class. He likely had many other women in his pocket he could ring. And he could see it, she knew. She wasn't ready to follow someone anywhere, all the time. She'd been following people her entire life. She didn't know where she was going next and didn't want to. The lack of decision was her decision.

When she didn't say anything else, Mateo said, "I'm gonna drop you off at Mavis's show. So you don't feel obligated to let me stay over for the night or anything like that. I can drive back."

Estelle wanted him to stay over but needed him to leave.

"Congratulations on the new life, seriously. Let me know how it turns out. I'm rooting for you." She nodded. He seemed earnest, not sarcastic. He opened the passenger door for her, and she got in. She watched him stuff his hands in his pockets and walk around the length of the car without looking back. They said nothing on the drive back to the gallery. When Mateo reached the entrance, the music was still banging; it grew into a large red mouth that could eat Estelle up if she surrendered. Estelle asked if Mateo wanted to go in and he shook his head. He took her hand, kissed the back of it, and said, "Good night, Estelle. I'll be around."

She got out of the car and watched him pull off into the wet, hot night. If she had stayed any longer in his car, she would have changed her mind, asked him to stay in her new room with her. She wanted all of these things, but she wasn't ready for them. She wanted to cry but didn't know why she should be sad. The Soft Space in her heart was silent.

That night, the band played, and Estelle and Mavis were bound hip-to-hip throughout the show. The main act was a saxophonist who reminded Estelle of the bluesman who had raised her and Mavis. This different man was in his forties, with skin as soft and brown as tilled earth. He played a song that made the Soft Space in Estelle's heart hum. She could see the notes fly from the cave of his instrument. They sunk in and stuck in her chest. She was still confused but, at the very least, alive.

Later that night, after Mavis did her rounds talking to the gallery folks, they went home. Mavis took a tarot card reader along with her, a friend of the main act, a pretty biracial girl with orange freckles and a chartreuse hairwrap. Mavis probably liked this girl and Estelle was glad Mavis would be occupied for the rest of the night. She didn't want to talk about Mateo, nor the House of Grace.

Inside the town house, Mavis smoked weed and sat at the kitchen table. The tarot reader offered to cut the cards. Estelle left them; she wanted to sleep or see the ocean. She couldn't tell which. She felt an ache for something filling and it hadn't come yet, and she wasn't sure how to get it. She talked to the Soft Space in her heart and paced in the hallway as Mavis and the reader mumbled along. Mavis heard Estelle's feet and called her over. Estelle wandered back in. Mavis had turned on the multicolored lights; the room was cloudy with pink and smelled like citrus.

Mavis plopped her hands on the table. She reached over and wrapped a loose arm around Estelle. "Stay here for a second, my girl. It's okay. You're doing fine."

Estelle suppressed the urge to weep.

The tarot reader finished shuffling the deck. She was about to do her work when Mavis plucked the first card. She slammed it on the table. It was the Hierophant, a wispy woman dressed in blue robes, clutching a cross. Estelle winced.

"I picked my sister," Mavis said. "I win a good future!"

"That's not how this works," the reader said. "That was a coincidence." She took the card back and shuffled again.

Estelle was too tired to know if she believed in those kinds of coincidences.

"It's just cards," Mavis laughed. "I just imbue my own meaning onto it. I'm calling this one my sister."

"There's a spiritual element to this," the reader said.

"There's a spiritual element to everything," Mavis said, "I'm a spiritual element. I am 'large and contain multitudes.'" She nodded at Estelle. "My girl used to be that card. I want to pick another and make this reading about her."

"What?" The tarot reader blew air from her nose. Estelle chuckled to herself. Mavis wasn't for everyone.

Mavis plucked her finger at Estelle. "I want that card."

"I'm going to start again. If you want to do a pick-a-card, I need the piles in threes. Don't touch it until I'm done." Mavis was already stoned but the weed hadn't affected the reader much.

"Gotcha. I'm going to win the next round with my new ace," Mavis drawled. She took another hit and passed it to the reader, who also took in a puff. The reader's arms relaxed.

Estelle didn't want to be involved. She went over to the hallway window and opened it. The air was angry and hot. Everything was too hot. She thought about Mateo. About Father Franco and Adriana and Bianca. She could hear the Soft Space in her heart sometimes; other times, it said nothing.

Mavis turned and called to Estelle.

"So now that you've felt all sorts of things," Mavis said, her eyes red-veined. "Leaving. Limerence. Lust. Love. What will you do tomorrow?"

Estelle shook her head. "I don't get you."

"There's another Liberation Day tomorrow. You'll choose new things to do," Mavis said, pushing her face close to the cards. "Every day you're free. Girl, you were always free."

Estelle lingered by Mavis. She stared at her sister, at her swan neck and black greased curls. She was beautiful, her true-kin.

"I want to see the ocean tonight."

Mavis reached into her pocket and produced her keys. "It's two blocks up, on the left. You'll see it."

Mavis grabbed Estelle's wrist, pulled it toward her. Estelle placed her free hand on Mavis's head and felt another kind of sweetness. Mavis looked at Estelle seriously and said, "Be careful. Come back soon."

Estelle nodded, and Mavis let her hand loose.

That night, Estelle left the town house. She padded over the grasses, slumped with condensation, and walked onto the shadowed street. The wind was wild and frustrated and stumbling and it rattled the neighbor's fences and gates. The Soft Space in Estelle's heart told her to keep going, keep going.

Estelle followed Mavis's directions until she saw a snatch of ocean, growling and panting black. She parted the grasses that grew over a foot-tramped path to the sea. The moon blazed, lit the gray sand until it glowed. She ran to the shoreline, sat down on the scattering sand. She watched the ocean. The wind kept acting rowdy and the ocean kept talking and laughing and whistling. The songs in Estelle's head joined the gibbering waves. Those songs sounded like everyone she'd ever met and would meet again. The waves, those voices, spoke and spoke. She heard the Soft Space in her heart and all the right voices, singing and singing, just enough music for one day.

Acknowledgments

Thank you to Abba, who is everything and all.

To Sonia McCauley, my mother, who is the reason I'm a writer, a woman, alive and well. You made me see life with brightness and hope, and you made me a reader. You are the reason I write; you are my heart.

To Jerry McCauley, who has guided me with his amazing mind and endless knowledge. I love you.

To Timothy McCauley, my best friend and brother, who has picked me up when I'm the lowest and still keeps me going on.

To LaKaléa McCauley, I'm so happy you are my brother's wife. You are a beautiful example of an exceptional Black woman who commands attention with your grace.

My dear family, everything I do is for you.

Thank you for nurturing me and caring for me; I live every day for you.

Thank you to Jesse Biehn, my dearest love, who supports me with unconditional devotion, reads my work with incredible attention, and stays by my side through everything with saintly patience. I'm amazed by you and fall in love with your heart over and over again, every day. I love you, forever.

Thank you to Joe Aires, my high school teacher who

made me want to become a writer. You mentored me and believed in me and always saw my future before I could see it. You are a gift.

Thank you to Amanda Jain, my agent, who has been in my corner for such a long time. I don't know what I'd do without you. You are a kindhearted, fiercely intelligent stalwart who makes dreams come true.

Thank you to Dan López, who is such a fantastic, responsive, and stunningly supportive editor who knew exactly how to gorgeously shape this work. I'm so lucky to have you as an editor.

To Jennifer Alton, who saw my work, stood up for it, and believed in it and me, who edited my story beautifully and gave this book life. I'm forever thankful for you.

To Dan Smetanka, who has been an incredible force, and to everyone at Counterpoint: Sarah Jean Grimm, Megan Fishmann, Rachel Fershleiser, Laura Berry, Yukiko Tominaga, Wah-Ming Chang, and Barrett Briske especially, who worked hard to get this book out in the world. Thank you to Nicole Caputo and Jaya Miceli for the beautiful cover. You all really saw me. Thank you so much for recognizing my vision for this project.

Thank you to those who gave me valuable commentary on this book. To Geeta Kothari, who read and edited "Last Saints" when I was a confused and nervous undergrad who thought having a book out was a dream too good to be true. Her class gave me the courage to be a writer. To Debra

Dean, whom I wrote "The Missing One" for in her gradu-
ate workshop; she has always seen my vision and encouraged
me endlessly, and I'm so fortunate that she was my incredible professor and treasured mentor over the years. To Lynne
Barrett, who had me write "Torsion" for her plot class and
basically shaped the whole thing through her prompts, and
who has been a major supporter of my work for a long time.
You are an amazing professor and writer, and I'm so blessed
to have been in your wonderful classes. To Je Banach, who
workshopped "Last Saints" and the first chapter of one of my
novels at the Yale Writer's Conference. You are such a powerful presence and so inspiring to me and to your students. To
Speer Morgan, who has also been my cherished mentor over
the years, who taught me how to be an editor and a fiction
writer and how to love the stories brimming in every person
you meet. I am forever indebted to you and your brilliance.
To Trudy Lewis, who knows how to find the heart of a story
and make it shine. Your humility, enlightened view of literature, and kindness are endlessly admirable to me, and I am
grateful for you. To Anand Prahlad, for making an indelible
mark on my life with your talent, love for your students, and
commitment to literature. Our conversations stay with me,
and I'm so fortunate you were my professor. To Sheri-Marie
Harrison, who made me want to be a professor after I saw
this badass, genius Black Caribbean woman in command of
her field, her work, and her life. To Mamadou Badiane, who
really understands the Afro-Latino experience and who gave

me exceptional commentary on my work. You are all so special to me. To Jacinda Townsend, who led a wonderful workshop at Kimbilio and showed me how to shape "La Espera."

Thank you to the wonderful Ivelisse Rodriguez, De'Shawn Charles Winslow, Margaret Wilkerson Sexton, and Deesha Philyaw for reading this book and exquisitely finding its core.

Thank you to Phong Nguyen, who has always been a great support and published "La Espera" when it was still "Esperando." I'm forever a fan. To Joe Clifford, who saw the value in "I Don't Know Where I'm Bound" and published it in his anthology. You're a rock star.

Thank you to Carol Ward, my other mother whose spirituality, love, talent, and sweetness have remained with me always. To Ashleigh Piini, my other sister, who has given me strength, to Joe Piini, who has been on my side, to Steve Biehn and Beth Biehn, who have been valued supporters of my work. To Sydney Spratte, who is a bright light, and to Brennan and Britni Spratte, who are lovely souls. To Marcia Biehn, who is a brilliant angel.

Thank you to my workshop groups at Yale Writer's Conference and my tribes at FIU, Mizzou, Kimbilio, and Canto Mundo, who have given me astonishing insights and have added immeasurably to my life. Thank you to my students, who always give me the energy to go forward.

Thank you to Uprise Bakery and Hitt Records in Columbia, Missouri, and to Soul Freak in Clear Lake Shores, Texas, for giving me beautiful spaces to write and edit this book. To the Del Toro Trio and Pierce, for giving me the soundtrack to edit this book. Rock on!

And thank you especially to you, the reader, for taking the time to go on this journey with my characters. I appreciate you with all my heart. Mil gracias.

Publication Acknowledgments

"Last Saints" in *First Inkling: Best of College Writing* anthology (SUNY Rockland), September 2012.

"Fevers" in *Gravel*, spring 2016.

"The Missing One" (published as "Bagmen") in *Jabberwock Review*, March 2017.

"I Don't Know Where I'm Bound" in *Just to Watch Them Die: Crime Fiction Inspired by the Songs of Johnny Cash* (Gutter Press), August 2017.

"Torsion" in *Vassar Review*, fall 2017.

"When Trying to Return Home" (published in poem form) in *Aspasiology*, January 2018.

"La Espera" (published as "Esperando") in *Pleiades*, January 2019.

© Jesse Biehn

JENNIFER MARITZA McCAULEY
is a writer, poet, and university professor. She has
been awarded fellowships from the National En-
dowment for the Arts, CantoMundo, Kimbilio,
and the Sundress Academy for the Arts. She holds
an MFA from Florida International University and
a PhD in creative writing and literature from the
University of Missouri. The author of the cross-
genre collection *SCAR ON/SCAR OFF*, she is an
assistant professor of literature and creative writing
at the University of Houston–Clear Lake.